Bev

W9-DFK-650

Harlequin
Presents..

Other titles by

ANNE MATHER
IN HARLEQUIN PRESENTS

#29 .... MONKSHOOD
#32 .... JAKE HOWARD'S WIFE
#35 .... SEEN BY CANDLELIGHT
#38 .... MOON WITCH
#41 .... DANGEROUS ENCHANTMENT
#46 .... PRELUDE TO ENCHANTMENT
#49 .... A SAVAGE BEAUTY
#54 .... THE NIGHT OF THE BULLS
#57 .... LEGACY OF THE PAST
#61 .... CHASE A GREEN SHADOW
#65 .... WHITE ROSE OF WINTER
#69 .... MASTER OF FALCON'S HEAD
#74 .... LEOPARD IN THE SNOW
#77 .... THE JAPANESE SCREEN
#86 .... RACHEL TREVELLYAN
#92 .... MASK OF SCARS
#96 .... SILVER FRUIT UPON SILVER TREES
#100 .... DARK MOONLESS NIGHT
#105 .... NO GENTLE POSSESSION
#110 .... WITCHSTONE
#112 .... THE WATERFALLS OF THE MOON
#119 .... PALE DAWN, DARK SUNSET

Many of these titles, and other titles in the
Harlequin Romance series, are available at your
local bookseller, or through the Harlequin Reader
Service. For a free catalogue listing all available
Harlequin Presents titles and Harlequin Romances,
send your name and address to:

HARLEQUIN READER SERVICE,
M.P.O. Box 707
Niagara Falls, N.Y. 14302

Canadian address:
Stratford, Ontario, Canada N5A 6W4
or use order coupon at back of books.

ANNE MATHER

sweet revenge

Harlequin Books

TORONTO • LONDON • NEW YORK • AMSTERDAM • SYDNEY • WINNIPEG

© Anne Mather 1970

Original hard cover edition published in 1970
by Mills & Boon Limited, 17 - 19 Foley Street,
London W1A 1DR, England.

SBN 373-70503-4

Harlequin Presents edition published May 1973

Second printing 1973
Third printing 1973
Fourth printing 1973
Fifth printing 1973
Sixth printing 1974
Seventh printing 1974
Eighth printing 1976

All the characters in this book have no existence outside the
imagination of the Author, and have no relation whatsoever to
anyone bearing the same name or names. They are not even
distantly inspired by any individual known or unknown to the
Author, and all the incidents are pure invention.

The Harlequin trade mark, consisting of the word HARLEQUIN
and the portrayal of a Harlequin, is registered in the United States
Patent Office and in the Canada Trade Marks Office.

Printed in Canada.

CHAPTER ONE

TONI MORLEY sipped the iced lemon juice, staring abstractedly at the mural of the beach at Estoril which adorned the walls of the small *restaurante*. She felt dejected and resentful, unwilling as yet to contact the airport with a view to booking a flight back to London. It hardly seemed possible that this time yesterday she had been a happy, carefree girl, revelling in her good fortune at having found a position so suited to her personality. How incredible it seemed that in twenty-four hours her whole outlook on life could be changed!

Ignoring the rather intimate glances she was receiving from the young Portuguese at the next table, she rummaged in her handbag for her cigarettes, and finding them lit one, drawing on it deeply. Her stomach still churned with indignation mixed with a natural sense of nervous tension, and she thrust her cigarettes away, straightening her shoulders almost involuntarily. After all, what had she to feel disturbed about? Why should she feel ashamed and unhappy when none of what had occurred had been her fault?

She swallowed another mouthful of lemon juice. Anyway, Pedro and Julia had not been the sweetest of children, spoilt as they undoubtedly were, yet they had possessed a certain charm, and Toni felt the familiar sense of despair overwhelm her as she realized and would no longer be there to look after them.

It was no good, she might as well admit it. This particular phase of her life was over, and there was nothing she could do to change that. All that should depress her was the knowledge that tomorrow at the very latest she must return to England and find herself another job.

She sighed. England. She had hoped to stay in Portugal for at least six months before returning to England. There was so much there to remind her of the small house in the suburbs, and the warmth and security of a happy home. A home that existed no more, except in the terms of a small bed-sitter in Kensington, her parents killed so suddenly and terribly in that pile-up on the M.1 only three months ago. This job, as nursery-governess to the two de Calle children, had seemed the ideal situation. She would live with the family in Lisbon, teaching the children who were six and four years, and escape entirely from memories of the past. Miguel de Calle, the children's father, was a business man, who travelled extensively, and Toni was to act also as a kind of companion for his wife, Estelle. The children would learn English, and later would attend an English school, and as Senhora de Calle was pregnant, Toni's own position seemed secure for several years.

Toni had been in Lisbon now for a little over three weeks, and had settled down very well. She had liked Estelle de Calle, and could discuss most things with her. Miguel de Calle had been away most of the time, on business in Spain and France, and had returned

6

home only three days ago. And that was the start of the trouble.

Toni stubbed out her cigarette, shivering a little in spite of the heat of the day. She was unused to scenes of any kind, and the kind of scene Estelle de Calle had created was completely beyond her comprehension. The Latin temperament, which she had seen little evidence of till then, had exploded with violent force, wreaking havoc with Toni's emotions. And over such a little thing . . .

She finished her lemon juice and rose to her feet. It was no good sitting here bemoaning her fate. She must return to London. What little money she had would pay her air fare back home to England, and then she would find herself another position forthwith. It was unfortunate that the de Calles had not yet paid her month's salary, for she doubted very much whether she would get that now.

She walked through the open swing doors of the *restaurante*, emerging into brilliant sunlight. She slid dark glasses on to her nose, and brushed back the heavy swathe of silvery blonde hair, smoothing it behind her ears. Then, swinging her handbag, she began to walk up the incline towards the narrower thoroughfare of the Avenue S. Maria. She had found a room this morning, in a small *pensão*, which would have to suffice until she was able to book her flight home.

Footsteps dogged her own, and glancing round apprehensively she found the young Portuguese from the *restaurante* was following her. Compressing her

7

lips, she deliberately quickened her step, only to find he quickened his step also, and presently came abreast of her, glancing at her sideways out of the corners of his lustrous dark eyes. '*Boa tarde, senhorita,*' he murmured, smiling intimately. 'Is something wrong?'

Toni considered whether to ignore him completely. Her knowledge of Portuguese was quite limited, and although he had spoken English she doubted whether his knowledge of her language was any greater than hers of Portuguese. Conversely, she had some small knowledge of the opposite sex, and such as it was it argued that to ignore him might encourage him to believe she was provocative. So she shook her head, and said: '*Não*' in a cold, aloof tone.

The boy merely continued to pace her and watch her intently. Toni looked about hopefully for a taxi. She hadn't a lot of money, it was true, but it would be the easiest way to rid herself of the young Portuguese's unwelcome attentions, without causing a scene, or involving anyone else. It was still some distance to the *pensão*, but she had no intention of allowing him to find out where she was staying.

'*Donde e qué e o Sr?*' the boy asked, moving closer so that his arm brushed hers.

Toni moved away to the kerb edge; she could not reply in Portuguese and he would not understand a rebuff in English, or if he did he would ignore it. She sighed. What was there about *her* that attracted such unwelcome attentions? First Miguel de Calle, and now this young boy. She doubted whether he was as old as she was.

He again moved nearer, almost forcing her off the pavement. She looked at him angrily, seeing the caressing lift of his eyes, and feeling an impotent sense of inadequacy. She looked round helplessly, and then saw the taxi coming from the opposite direction. Preoccupied with thoughts of escape, she did not stop to consider that there might be other traffic on the road. She stepped off the pavement, right into the path of a huge grey limousine. There was a scream of brakes as the driver of the car wrenched his wheel round desperately to avoid her. Toni felt the nearside wing brush her hip and she was thrown back on to the kerb, bruising her thigh on its lip, and lying there for a moment, stunned.

She became aware of the chatter of excited foreign voices, as a small crowd gathered and she made to get shakily to her feet. She was barely conscious that the driver of the limousine had extracted himself from behind the wheel of the car, slamming the door with savage impatience. He strode over to the group, thrusting the sightseers aside arrogantly, and almost hauling Toni to her feet with hard angry hands. Toni registered that he was a very dark man, with a thin tanned face that was marred by an ugly white scar that ran almost the full length of his left cheek, giving him a strangely satanic appearance, which was enhanced by the fury he was venting on her.

'*Deus!*' he ground out, glaring at her. '*Esta maluco?*'

Toni ran a hand over her forehead, gathering her scattered wits. 'I – I am English, *senhor*,' she said with difficulty. 'I am sorry if I startled you!'

9

'Sorry! You are *sorry!*' He glanced round angrily, dismissing the crowd by his expression. '*Senhorita,* are you in the habit of trying to kill yourself?'

Toni shivered, overcome with the realization of what had almost happened. 'I – I've said I'm sorry, *senhor,*' she said, swallowing hard. 'You must know I was not trying to kill myself.'

He released her shoulders and straightened. 'That may be so, *senhorita,* nevertheless, you almost succeeded! In future I would advise you to take a little more care when crossing our roads!'

He spoke with only a slight accent, and his voice was deep and attractive, but Toni was in no mood to appreciate this. Instead, he seemed to her the epitome of everything she had encountered since coming to Portugal: male arrogance, omnipotence and ignorance. She managed to move slightly away from him, wondering where the young Portuguese had disappeared to, and yet feeling a sense of relief that he had done so.

'If – if you will – excuse me—' she began, but he seemed to remember his own part in the proceedings, and to her astonishment, he said:

'Come, *senhorita.* As you are obviously a stranger in my country I will see that you reach your hotel without further incident.'

'Oh, no!' Toni shook her head, backing away. 'Thank you, but no!'

'I insist!' His tone was forceful, and the few sightseers who were left watched with amusement at this obvious battle of the sexes.

'And so do I,' exclaimed Toni. 'Good lord, do all

Portuguese refuse to take no for an answer?'

He shrugged, his dark eyes narrowed, and she thought inconsequently that he was the most attractive man she had ever encountered. He was not handsome in the accepted sense of the word, but he was tall and lean, and moved with a lithe fluid grace that suggested he was very fit. Only his scar detracted from his appearance, and yet it also added a kind of hard cynicism which was in itself a challenge. Remembering Miguel de Calle's soft hands and slightly over-fed body, Toni felt a sense of revulsion, as she compared him to this man who was regarding her with something like contempt in his eyes.

'Very well, *senhorita*. I will leave you to yourself, as this is what you wish!'

Toni flushed, feeling uncomfortable, and then, seeing a familiar face on the fringes of the group, changed her mind. '*Senhor*,' she began, as he turned away, 'I – I – could I take you up on your suggestion?'

The man studied her almost insolently for a moment, making Toni wish she had not spoken, and then gave a lift to his broad shoulders. 'As you wish.'

Toni nodded, and followed him to the smooth limousine with trembling legs. She felt the eyes of the young Portuguese following her from his position at the edge of the crowd, and slid into the car with relief. At least with this man she felt reasonably safe, although why she should do so, she couldn't imagine. In his way he could be eminently more dangerous.

As she entered the car she noticed a crest on the door; a silver shield emblazoned with scarlet lettering,

11

but the door was closed on her before she had a chance to read the words. She wondered what it meant, who he was, and then lay back in her seat with a feeling of defeat. She felt tired and weary and strangely near to tears.

The man walked round the bonnet and slid in beside her, his eyes meeting hers for a moment before he started the engine. Toni felt hot all over suddenly, and she twisted the strap of her handbag nervously. It was a long time since any man had disturbed her as this man did, just by looking at her with those incredibly black eyes. She noticed that his lashes were long also, thick and dark, like his hair, which grew rather low on his neck providing a contrast to the brilliant whiteness of his shirt. His suit was dark too, and immaculate, and Toni thought it very likely that it was only one of many. The car, too, was immaculate, a continental luxury sports car with a speedometer that reached fantastic speeds.

He glanced her way once more, and Toni's colour deepened as she realized he had been aware of her scrutiny.

'Your hotel, *senhorita*,' he murmured softly. 'Its location?'

Toni swallowed her breath, choked, recovered and said: 'Er – the *Rua S. Henriques*, it's a *pensão* actually!'

'Ah!' He nodded, and swung the car into a thickly trafficked area, letting the wheel slide through his fingers with lazy expertise. Toni put her head on one side, as crazy thoughts flitted through her mind. So, too, would he make love, she thought; expertly, his hard, lean hands arousing passionate response. She allowed herself a slight smile at her thoughts, and then caught her bottom lip between her teeth as he became aware of her amusement and quelled it with a glance.

'You find something amusing, *senhorita*?' he asked coolly.

Toni shook her head. 'No, not amusing, *senhor*.'

He concentrated on his driving, and Toni saw the sign for the *Rua S. Henriques* with a sense of regret which she could not understand. Then the car halted at the door of the *pensão* and she slid out quickly, not waiting for his assistance which he had walked round politely to offer.

'Th – thank you, *senhor*,' she murmured awkwardly. 'I'm sorry for being such a nuisance!'

He shook his head. 'It was nothing, *senhorita*. However, I would suggest you should not encourage our youths too freely.'

Toni stared at him. Had he been aware of what had happened all along? He gave a lazy smile, and with a slight bow he slid back into the automobile, leaving Toni with the feeling of his having amused himself at her expense.

Clenching her fists, she turned, and walked angrily into the *pensão*. It was too late to make arrangements to leave now. She would have to wait until the morning when she might feel more normal. Just now, she felt upset and unhappy, and not a little disturbed.

An hour later, showered and changed into a slim-fitting suit of blue poplin, she left the *pensão* again in search of a meal. The evening air was warm and sweet-smelling, coffee blending with the more subtle scents of the flowers. She refused to admit that she was loath to make any definite arrangements to leave Lisbon. There was something about the place that had enchanted her, and she hated the idea of returning to the drab greys of London's suburbs. Here there was so much life and colour, so much to interest one who found history so enthralling.

Leaving the *Rua S. Henriques* she walked towards the river down a street lined with coloured houses, looking like boxes of candy set in flower beds. Wherever she walked in Lisbon she found something new to delight her, up and down its ancient hills where church spires stood like sentinels against the skyline. Staying with the de Calles, she had taken the children everywhere, visiting the quays and public squares, the parks and museums. Julia, who was only four, had soon tired of sightseeing, but Pedro, with his active, intelligent mind, had shared her interest and she had enjoying sharing it with him.

She entered a small park, in the centre of which was a tinkling fountain, sparkling, the sun casting the drops in a thousand different shades of colour. She sat on its rim, watching the young mothers and nannies parading their children, some in perambulators, others walking, tiny tots in frilly dresses with ribbons in their hair. She wondered whether there was any chance of her getting another job in Portugal. It did not seem likely when the de Calles refused to give her a reference.

A young man came and sat near her on the rim of the fountain, and Toni hunched her shoulders irritatedly. Surely she was not going to have to contend with yet another awkward situation? She rose to go, but the young man rose simultaneously and they faced one another.

'Toni!'

'Paul!'

Toni stared at Paul Craig with more warmth than she would have normally shown, but it was so nice to see a familiar face. Not that Paul's face looked particularly English, for he was dark-haired and dark-skinned, though not so dark as the man she had met that afternoon she had to concede, but at least he was a friend. Meanwhile Paul was smiling at her. 'Toni Morley!' he was saying. 'What are you doing in Portugal?'

'I *was* working,' said Toni ruefully.

'Was? Why? What's happened? Have you lost your job?'

'Something like that,' remarked Toni dryly, without enlarging on it. She thought Paul's smile was rather forced, and said: 'Are you on holiday?'

'Sort of.' Paul shook his head. 'It's a long story. Look, why don't we have a drink together? I mean, for old times' sake. It's good to see you again, Toni.'

Toni was reluctant. 'Oh, I don't know, Paul—' Her association with Paul Craig had been short-lived, and she had no desire to revive it.

'Oh, come on, Toni. Ships that pass in the night, and all that sort of jazz. Strangers in a foreign city. Come on – no strings, honestly.'

Toni shrugged. 'Okay, Paul. Just one, then. How have you been?'

'Fine. How about you?'

'Oh, fine.' Toni glanced his way thoughtfully as they walked out of the park and across the road to a bar. Paul didn't change much. He had always seemed rather boyish, and Toni had soon tired of being treated like one of his rugger chums. He liked sport, and nights out with the 'boys' and Toni had never taken him seriously, much to his disgust.

They sat at a long dimly lit bar, on high stools, drinking martini cocktails. Paul offered her a cigarette, and after they were lit, he said:

'Did you know I was engaged?'

'No!' Toni half-smiled. 'Who's the lucky girl?'

Paul grimaced. 'Janet West, as was. We broke it off today.'

'What!'

'Yes. We were here together. We were going to see my grandmother. But – well – Janet's damn extravagant, she's always wanting money for something or other, and then yesterday she went and spent over two thousand escudos on an evening dress!'

'I see. And you objected.'

'You're damn right I objected!' He drew on his cigarette angrily. 'Then she just blew it all in. This morning I got back the ring.'

'That's a shame, Paul.' Toni sipped her drink. 'Are you completely brokenhearted?'

Paul snorted. 'Not likely! I've had enough of her for some considerable time!'

'Oh, come on! You're only mad now. You'll come round.' Toni smiled.

Paul shook his head. 'I doubt it. Anyway, what gives with you? What are you doing wandering alone about a foreign city at night?'

'It's hardly night yet.' Toni shrugged. 'Oh, it's rather complicated, Paul. You wouldn't be interested.'

'I might be.'

'Well—' Toni ran the tips of her fingers round the rim of her glass. 'Well – I came out to act as governess to two young children, Pedro and Julia de Calle.'

'Did you say *de Calle*?'

'Yes. Why? Do you know them?'

'My grandmother does. But go on. I'm sorry I interrupted you.'

Toni sipped her cocktail. 'Perhaps as you know the de Calles it would be better if I stopped right here.'

'They're my grandmother's friends, not mine. Do go on, Toni.'

'All right. Well, everything was going swimmingly, until Miguel de Calle came back from his business trip. Then I guess he took a fancy to me. Don't ask me why, I didn't encourage him.'

'Honey, with your looks, men don't need encouragement,' remarked Paul fervently.

Toni gave him an old-fashioned look, and then continued: 'Naturally, I wasn't aware of it until he cornered me one night in the corridor outside my bedroom. Lord, I really thought I was to suffer a fate worse than death, and I was practically tearing his hair out when Senhora de Calle came upon us. Of

17

course she thought the opposite to the truth: that I had been trying to seduce Miguel. I denied it all, of course, but to no avail, and this morning I found myself out on my ear, bluntly speaking. That pig, Miguel, I could murder him! He stood by and let Estelle rant and rave at me, looking like the wounded soldier!' Her angry young voice was filled with hurt and resentment, and Paul slid an arm across her shoulders.

'Poor you! So what are you going to do now?'

'Do? Well, return to London, I guess. There's nothing else I can do. The de Calles haven't even paid me, let alone given me a reference!'

'I see.' Paul nodded, studying his drink. 'I'm not sure what I'm doing either.'

'But I thought you were going to visit your grandmother.'

'I said Janet and I were going to visit her,' amended Paul.

'So?'

'So I can't go alone.'

Toni looked exasperated. 'Why?'

'Well, because so far I've been classed as the black sheep of the family, the only one unmarried and so forth. When she heard of my engagement to Janet she was overjoyed, and that's how we got this invitation. She'll be furious when she finds out it's all over.'

'Well, it wasn't your fault!' said Toni reasonably.

'You try telling her that!' Paul looked disgruntled. 'She's been trying to marry me off for years.'

'Well, maybe you'll make it up with Janet after all.'

'I doubt it. She won't even speak to me.'

'I see.' Toni smiled gently. 'I guess we'd better make that a double booking back to London!'

Paul chewed at his lip. 'I was looking forward to the break. Estrada, that's where my grandmother lives, is a beautiful place, on the coast. It's an estate, actually.'

'How come your grandmother is Portuguese?' asked Toni curiously.

'My mother was Portuguese,' said Paul. 'She ran away with my father when she was just eighteen, and for a while the rest of her family ignored her. They were scandalized. They had a nice arranged marriage lined up for her. Anyway, when my grandfather died, my grandmother had second thoughts and she forgave my mother. There was a grand reconciliation, you know the sort of thing, and then I was produced for their inspection, and I guess my grandmother thought she would try and run my life as she failed with my mother's.'

'Sounds pretty old-fashioned,' said Toni, frowning.

'Well, I guess it is. Things go on the same here for hundreds of years.'

'Well, thank goodness I'm not Portuguese, then,' said Toni, with some enthusiasm.

'It can be pleasant, for a woman,' remarked Paul thoughtfully. 'I mean – what you gain on the round-abouts you lose on the swings, sort of thing. In England women have achieved independence, equality, and so on, but they've lost a lot of their femininity doing it.'

'Oh, come on!' Toni stared at him. 'What's all this

leading up to?'

Paul gave a reluctant smile. 'Very little really. I wondered whether you'd agree to come to Estrada with me. As my fiancée.'

Toni stared at him. 'I could *what*?'

'Oh, in name only,' Paul hastened to add. 'Just as a favour to me, that's all. It would save a lot of explanations that I don't want to have to give. And you wouldn't have to return to England without having a holiday.'

'Oh, Paul! I couldn't do a thing like that!'

'Why? Why not? Where's the harm?'

'Well, I wouldn't like to deceive your grandmother like that.'

'Why?' Paul gave an exasperated shake of his head. 'I mean, there's nothing to harm anyone. You could be my fiancée, quite easily, if we hit it off together.' Then as Toni sought about for words to say, he went on: 'Oh, I know it's not on. Our engagement, I mean. But all I'm trying to show you is that it could be true, without any questions asked.'

Toni sighed. 'Yes, I can see that. But, Paul, it isn't so imperative that you produce a fiancée, is it? I mean, you could go alone and face the music.'

'I could,' he agreed, bending his head. 'But my grandmother is not a young woman, and I don't like disappointing her.'

Toni reserved judgment there. Pleasant though Paul might be, he didn't strike her as the kind of young man to worry a great deal about his grandmother's feelings unless they directly concerned him.

'And what would happen if I agreed to your schemes and went with you to Estrada and we weren't found out? I mean, your family, in Portugal anyway, would expect you to marry me, and when you didn't it would be just as bad as breaking your engagement to Janet.'

'I know. But I'd arrange for that to be revealed long after my return to England when I'd be many miles away from the storm.' Paul smiled. 'Look, Toni, I've looked forward to this holiday for a long time, and if I turn up there now, without Janet, I'll have to spend the whole holiday explaining my actions and trying to make amends.'

Toni grimaced. 'I'm sure you're exaggerating, Paul.'

He half-smiled. 'Not much, believe me! Anyway, what have you to lose?'

'Nothing. It's not that. It would probably be marvellous.'

'Well, then!'

'What if Janet does come back? What if she comes to the estate?'

'She won't,' said Paul, with some confidence. 'She'll expect me to run after her, as I usually do. Only this time I've had it, right up to here.' He raised his hand to the level of his chin.

Toni glanced at her watch. 'It's no good, Paul. I've got to go.'

'Toni, *please*! Won't you change your mind?'

'How can I? I'm not the type for intrigue.'

'But what intrigue is there going to be? I mean,

heavens, even if we are found out, it's not the end of the world.'

Toni sighed, looking at him thoughtfully. Just why was she refusing such an opportunity? What had she got to lose, after all? If Paul wanted to pretend she was his fiancée and it was the means to a marvellous extension of her brief stay in Portugal why should she object? She shook her head. In spite of her natural revulsion at playing at being Paul's fiancée there was much to commend the scheme. Only some inner sense of perception warned her that the situation might not be as simple as he would have her believe.

But despite all these doubts, the temptation was there. The way Paul put it, his fiancée could be anybody, and so long as she could get used to being called Janet, and let Paul make all the leading moves, she could not see that anything could go wrong.

'You make it sound so easy,' she exclaimed.

'It is easy,' he insisted. 'What have you got to look forward to back in London? Probably the usual wet summer weather English people come abroad to escape. You've not got another job waiting, so you're not losing any money. This will be a free holiday before you need to start looking for another job. I don't know of any other girl who would turn it down.'

'Nor do I,' murmured Toni, finishing her drink.

Paul beckoned the barman and ordered two more drinks, and then said:

'Where are you staying?'

'A *pensão* in the *Rua S. Henriques*,' said Toni slowly.

'Good. That's not far from where I'm staying. I could pick you up in the morning—'

'Hold on, hold on,' she exclaimed. 'I haven't said I'll come yet.'

'But you will, won't you?'

Toni studied him. 'If – and I say only *if* – I decide to come, you won't at any time attempt to turn this mild deception into the real thing, will you?'

Paul's cheeks reddened. 'Of course not.' He hunched his shoulders. 'Anyway, why am I so repugnant to you all of a sudden?'

'You're not repugnant to me, Paul. It's not that. It's just that we aren't at all suited to one another. I like you – but I could never love you.'

'All right, all right. You don't have to rub it in,' said Paul sulkily. 'Now to details . . .'

Toni sighed. 'No, wait! Give me time to think about it. I can't just decide in a moment. This is a big thing for me. Besides, if I disappear into the interior of Portugal with a strange male the agency in London who employed me in the first place are going to think it mighty peculiar when this Senhora de Calle lets them know I've been dismissed for attempted seduction, and I haven't even made an appearance.'

'Does that matter? I mean, there are heaps of agencies in London.'

'Y-e-s,' said Toni doubtfully. 'Oh, Paul, I wish I could just go as a friend or something.'

Paul grimaced. 'Heavens, I never thought you were a prig!'

'I'm not – that is – oh, all right, all right. I'll give it

a try. It will be a bit of an adventure anyway. You swear this grandmother of yours won't be calling in the preacher as soon as we arrive?'

Paul laughed, half with relief, Toni thought wonderingly. 'No, of course not. So long as I'm engaged, that will be as good as the real thing for her.'

Toni felt sceptical, and then shook away the twinges of conscience that pricked her. She was not by nature a deceitful girl, and only the longing to stay a little longer in this enchanting country had tipped the scales in Paul's direction.

CHAPTER TWO

THEY drove east from Lisbon the following morning, passing through some of the most beautiful countryside Toni had ever seen. She would have liked to have taken the journey in easy stages, exploring as she went, but Paul obviously had only his destination in mind, and so she kept silent. For a while they followed the west bank of the Tagus, the sprawling river which provides a natural boundary to the city of Lisbon, before turning north towards Oporto.

Paul had told her that the *quinta*, which is the Portuguese word for estate, occupied a huge stretch of land bordering the coast in places, then stretching inland to where the vineyards flourished on the terraces above the Douro river. As he enlarged upon his family's affairs Toni ventured to ask:

'Does your grandmother have a manager to run the estate for her?'

Paul lifted his shoulders for a moment, as though finding it difficult to answer her, and then he said: 'Well, a manager does run the estate – but – well, Toni, my grandmother doesn't *own* the estate. It's a family concern that passes down from father to son.'

Toni frowned. 'But your mother – I mean – I thought your mother was your grandmother's only offspring.'

'I'm sorry if I misled you,' said Paul swiftly, although

Toni had the feeling that he wasn't sorry at all. 'My mother had a brother, my Uncle Raoul. Naturally, he now owns the estate.'

'I see.' Toni moved restlessly. 'I think you'd better tell me some more about this family of yours. All you appear to have revealed to me are the things they know about your ex-fiancée. It would be a good idea if I learned what Janet knew about them.'

Paul pulled out his cigarettes, and said: 'Light me one, Toni.' Then he grimaced. 'I didn't want to confuse you, that's all. I mean, there isn't a lot to know.' He took the lighted cigarette she handed him. 'My uncle lives at the house, of course. He's a widower. He has a daughter, Francesca, she's thirteen, I believe.'

Toni stared at him. 'Go on. Who else lives at the *quinta*?' Her voice was cool, and Paul looked exasperated.

'Stop getting so edgy!' he exclaimed. 'After all, it's no worse that meeting any other family.'

Toni reserved judgment. From what little she had learned of Portuguese families, they seemed far more severe than any English family. But it was a glorious morning, and soon she forgot her anxieties in the wonder of exclaiming at the vista spread out before them. They passed rivers and streams meandering gently in the dappled shade of fragrant pinewoods, they drove through villages where every cottage was painted a different pastel shade, blending in with the profusion of green foliage and brilliantly coloured flowers. Toni saw camellias growing wild in creamy disorder, while there were periwinkles and magnolias in abundance, spreading a carpet of perfume before them. The morning air was intoxicating and for a while Toni was content.

They stopped for lunch at an inn from where they could look down to the coast. While they ate fish stew and crusty bread rolls served by the innkeeper's buxom wife who didn't speak a word of English, Paul began to talk again about Estrada. He seemed to want to tell her something, and Toni again felt those twinges of apprehension.

'What's wrong?' she asked, sipping her wine. 'What is it you haven't told me?'

Paul flushed. 'I didn't say there was anything,' he hedged.

'I know. But I can tell there is something wrong, and it can only be to do with this affair.'

'Well, it's nothing much, Toni, really. But – well, my grandmother is a Dowager Condessa.'

'What!' Toni was incredulous. 'A Condessa! So this means that your uncle . . .' Her voice trailed away.

'Yes. My uncle is Conde Raoul della Maria Estrada.'

'I see.' Toni gave an involuntary shake of her head. 'And you really think we can get away with it? In these circumstances?'

'Why not?' Paul's voice gathered confidence when Toni did not immediately collapse at his revelations.

'Well,' Toni shrugged, 'I should imagine a Count is rather more particular about the girl his nephew is going to marry.'

'And?'

'I'm not the type! I mean – honestly, Paul, I thought

this was going to be so easy – your words, not mine – and every few miles you spring some new situation on me. Why didn't you explain everything at the beginning and then I could have refused right away?'

Paul lay back in his chair, his face petulant. 'I could have let you make the whole journey without telling you,' he said sulkily. 'I think you're behaving ridiculously. Are you coming or aren't you?'

'No, I'm not.' Toni shrugged. 'As to the rest of what you said, you know very well you couldn't have allowed me to arrive at Estrada without telling me the truth. I suppose you didn't tell me before now because you knew what my reactions might be. Heavens, when you said your grandmother knew the de Calles I might have known she wasn't as ordinary as you'd have had me believe.'

Paul shrugged. 'Well, so what! What has changed, actually? The *quinta* is still there, as it has always been, my grandmother is still an old lady with a desire to see me married before she dies. I can't see anything to get alarmed about.'

'Maybe you can't, but I can. Look, Paul, I've got no desire to spend a holiday with the aristocracy. I'd hate to have to behave formally all the time, it wouldn't be like a holiday!'

Paul frowned. 'They're not all that formal.'

'Oh no? I know just how formal Portuguese families can be!'

'So we go back.'

'I guess so. I'm sorry, Paul.'

'So am I, extremely sorry,' he muttered dejectedly.

Toni felt ungrateful. After all, it would have been wonderful in other circumstances. 'Paul—' she began, when Paul sprang to his feet, as an elderly man approached them.

'Tio Joachim!' he exclaimed. 'How good it is to see you!'

The man smiled benignly, and Toni swallowed hard. Paul's uncle it was, but not Uncle Raoul. And then, to her astonishment, Paul said:

'Tio Joachim, I want you to meet Janet, my fiancée, Janet darling, this is my great-uncle Joachim, Grandmother's youngest brother!'

Toni hesitated only a moment, casting a baleful glance at Paul, and then she rose too, and allowed the introductions to continue. There was little she could do about it, short of calling Paul a liar, and her innate sense of decency would not allow her to disgrace him in that way in front of his uncle. So she replied politely to Uncle Joachim's questions, behaving as Janet West, Paul's fiancée.

Joachim Vallarez did not stay long. He was merely passing through on his way to Coimbra, and the inn was his usual port of call. He was a harmless, charming old man, without any undue curiosity about his great-nephew's affairs, and in consequence Toni had plenty of time to think of answers to his questions. She had to attune herself to being an office worker, which was what Paul had told her Janet was, instead of remaining the governess she was used to. Otherwise it was perfectly simple, so long as she answered to the name of Janet.

After the old man had left, Paul looked rather smug. 'Well, you did it,' he said, lighting a cigarette. 'You had me sweating for a minute, but you didn't let me down. I thought you did admirably!'

Toni compressed her lips for a moment. 'I hadn't much choice, had I? Short of calling you a liar?'

'No, you hadn't. I banked on your not doing that!' He gave a short laugh. 'Uncle Joachim will tell my grandmother all about you, if you still insist we go back. It will upset her terribly if she thinks we've been in the district without visiting her.'

'I know, I know!' Toni put her hands over her ears for a second. 'All right, Paul, you win. I'll go on with it. Just don't push me too far, that's all.'

They arrived at Estrada in the late afternoon. They had been passing through the Estrada lands for some time, approaching the coastline all the way. Here the coast was strewn with tiny bays and inlets, coves yellow with sand, lapped by the azure blue waters of the Atlantic. Toni couldn't deny the surge of well-being she was feeling, and even the prospect of meeting a Dowager Condessa couldn't douse her enthusiasm.

Then, as they began the approach to the home of the della Maria Estradas, she caught her breath in amazement. Ahead of them, among pine trees, looking like a fairy-tale palace, was a small, exquisite castle, turreted and moated, its grey stone walls turning a faint pink in the glow of the afternoon sun.

'Oh, Paul,' she gasped. 'This surely can't be—'

'Yes. The Castelo Estrada! Do you like it?'

'But you never told me. . . .' Her voice trailed away.

'I suppose I ought to have known that something like this was at the end of it.' She thought cynically of the unknown Janet and her desire for riches. 'It's a pity Janet couldn't have seen this. She would certainly not have quarrelled with you then.'

'Yes.' Paul sounded thoughtful. 'However, beautiful places and beautiful things are of little use to Janet, or me, for that matter.'

Toni glanced at him, frowning. 'What do you mean?'

Paul snorted sardonically. 'It surely must have crossed even your mind that to maintain a castle in this day and age takes money, plenty of money!'

Toni screwed up her nose. 'That sounds mercenary, Paul.'

'I know. It was meant to.'

'Do you mean that if this – castle – was yours, you would sell it?' Her tone was incredulous.

'Well, maybe not if I had Uncle Raoul's income, but certainly if I were left the castle on a pittance, it would have to go. I'm no sentimentalist, Toni. As I've said, I get enjoyment from spending money, not looking at it!'

Toni did not reply. She thought Paul was very immature in some ways. With her innate love of beauty in all things, she couldn't understand the kind of mentality that could discount a building so mellowed with historical age in favour of money to be spent having a good time. In any case, she thought dryly, Paul's ideas of having a good time and her own were doubtless divergent.

The car swept up a long, gravelled drive. Before the

impressive façade of the castle it widened into a court-yard, while a narrow bridge spanned the moat and led into the inner recesses of the castle. The portcullis was no longer in use, but Toni, with her vivid imagination, could well picture the scene as it had once appeared to weary travellers, newly arrived in the country. The castle was placed in a strategic position, with the hills above providing a natural defence against unwary attack behind, and the sea in front.

The car negotiated the bridge, and they were in the courtyard, with Paul turning off the car's engine, and glancing encouragingly at Toni. Toni felt nervousness assail her, but she climbed out of the car swiftly, not allowing herself to think. There was no one about, and she looked at Paul, questioningly.

'Siesta,' replied Paul, in explanation. 'Afternoons are pretty quiet around here.'

'I see,' Toni nodded, and bent to lift her handbag out of the car. As she did so she became aware that they were being observed by a young girl, standing in the shadows of a huge oaken door. She was mostly in shadow, but Toni thought she looked about fourteen. Then she remembered. This would probably be Francesca, the Conde's daughter.

'Paul,' she murmured, looking at him and moving her head slightly in the child's direction.

Paul looked round. Then he nodded, and after lifting the cases out of the boot, he straightened and looking across at the girl, said: 'Hello, Francesca! Aren't you coming to greet us?'

Francesca moved her shoulders indolently, and came

reluctantly out of her hiding place. Now, in the sunlight, Toni could see she was very dark-skinned, her hair long and black and plaited into a single braid. Dressed in a short flared skirt and a white blouse, slip-on sandals on her bare feet, she could have been any one of the young peasant girls they had encountered on their journey from Lisbon. Her face was quite attractive, but it had a petulant expression, and Toni thought with a feeling of apprehension that Francesca might prove to be more intimidating than her grandmother. She looked as though she was used to having her own way, and as she was the only child in a house governed by an elderly relation she was very probably thoroughly spoilt.

Thrusting aside these uncharitable thoughts, Toni smiled at her now, but there was no answering smile, and instead Francesca put her hands on her hips, and said insolently:

'You were supposed to be here yesterday, *primo* Paul.'

Her English was very good, and Toni glanced at Paul to see what his reaction to this might be.

He merely shrugged and said: 'As my grandmother is the only person to whom I must excuse myself I don't think that remark was called for, Francesca. I see your manners don't improve.'

Francesca wrinkled her nose rudely, and turned away. Toni felt uncomfortable, even though Francesca was only a precocious child, and Paul, sensing this, said: 'Francesca! Kindly tell José we are here, and that the bags need seeing to. Would you also tell Luisa, and

33

before you start giving me some more lip I should warn you that any more of it will find you being reported to your father – understood?'

Francesca shrugged her shoulders. 'My father is away, so you would be disappointed,' she retorted.

'He'll return,' returned Paul smoothly. 'Now, jump to it!'

Francesca looked as though she might argue, but then she turned and went through the heavy door into the building.

'Charming,' said Toni dryly. 'Is she a sample of what I'm to expect?'

Paul chuckled. 'No, of course not. Francesca doesn't like it when I come here. She's a very possessive child, and when her father's away, as he often is, she monopolizes our grandmother's time. As we are the only grandchildren, naturally her nose is a little put out when I'm here.'

'I see.' Toni shook her head. 'I suppose when her father is around you're not quite such a nuisance.'

Paul nodded. 'Something like that,' he conceded. 'When Raoul's here no one else exists. She adores him. She's terribly jealous. I guess the fact that she never knew her mother is mainly responsible.'

'She didn't know her mother? Why?'

'She died when Francesca was only three years old. Naturally, she was too young to remember much about her. She had a nanny, you see, and only saw her mother at certain times of the day. Portuguese noblewomen don't spend a great deal of time in the nursery, you know.'

Toni raised her eyebrows. 'They miss a lot, then. If, or when, I have children, I intend to care for them my-self, whatever my circumstances.'

Paul laughed. 'Well, not all women are interested in their children, you know.'

–'I know,' Toni sighed. 'But it seems wrong to dele-gate a woman's natural instincts to someone else. I guess I'm old-fashioned.'

Paul smiled. 'Maybe you are. Maybe it's a good thing. I'm sure Grandmother will think so. She never got on with Elise.'

'Elise? Oh, was that your uncle's wife?'

'Yes. She was French. Anyway, we can talk about that at some other time. Let's go in.'

They entered by the west door into a high arched hall, which Toni realized immediately was the main hall of the castle. The stone walls were hung with wall tapestries, while there was a huge coat of arms em-blazoning the wall above the fireplace. A carved wooden staircase was at the end of the hall and this led on to a gallery which ran the length of the hall. The stone floor had been highly polished and strewn with heavy colour-ful rugs, some of skin, that blended in perfectly with their surroundings. The furniture was all carved wood, heavy and completely in keeping with the rest of the decorations. Toni thought it was very beautiful, but not exactly luxurious. The lighting was provided by electric candelabra, set in sconces about the walls, and it seemed altogether medieval. She thought it was likely that the Conde, Paul's uncle, kept it this way purposely, when others might have tried to modernize it.

Paul was looking at her interestedly. 'Feudal, isn't it?' he remarked dryly. 'But don't be alarmed, it's not all like this.'

Then two people appeared, followed rather more slowly by Francesca. Toni guessed they must be José and Luisa. José was quite old, but Luisa was a middle-aged Portuguese, dressed completely in black, her skirts longer than any Toni had ever seen. To complete the picture, a bunch of keys hung from her belt, and Toni had to hide the smile that sprang to her lips.

Paul spoke warmly to José as he passed on his way to get their suitcases, and then greeted Luisa enthusiastically.

'Janet,' he said, after he had spoken a few words of Portuguese to Luisa, 'this is Luisa. She's a veritable treasure. Not only does she supervise the servants with a will of iron, but she cooks like an angel! Luisa, *este e minha noiva* Janet West.'

Luisa smiled politely, gave a half-curtsey, and said: 'It is a pleasure to meet you, *senhorita*. I hope you will enjoy your stay at the *castelo*. If you will come with me, I will show you to your room. *Senhor*, will you wait for José? He will take your baggage to your quarters.'

Paul agreed, and gave Toni another encouraging wink. 'See you later, Janet,' he said, lightly, and so casually that Toni wondered whether he was used to intrigue. 'Come down when you're ready. Luisa will tell you where. Tell me, before you go, Luisa, how is my grandmother?'

Luisa lifted her shoulders eloquently. 'As well as can be expected, *senhor*,' she replied. 'She has had a little more trouble with her heart – and some rheumatics, but otherwise she continues quite well.' Toni felt relieved. If a servant could speak of the Condessa with such warmth in her voice she could not be so formidable.

She followed Luisa up the staircase and along the gallery, her eyes wide with enthusiasm. There was so much to see. The walls of the gallery were lined with portraits of previous Condes of Estrada, their features dark and forbidding, their clothes made of silks and satins, slashed with vivid colours. Toni stared at them curiously, hardly aware of Luisa's remarks concerning their journey, and the heat of the day. They passed through an arched doorway into a wide corridor and now Toni saw what Paul had said earlier. Here the floors were mosaic-tiled, which without detracting from the decor, nevertheless permitted a slight trend towards modernization. The stone walls had been panelled with rich dark wood, and tiny windows had been enlarged to let in more light.

They followed the corridor for some way before branching off to their left along another corridor. Toni tried to remember these turnings. She was trying to keep her bearings in relation to the great hall. At last Luisa halted before a white panelled door, and flinging it open said:

'Your rooms, *senhorita*!'

Toni stepped inside on to cool marble tiles, strewn as downstairs with soft, furry rugs. The shutters had been released from her windows, and a faint breeze from the sea stole through the open windows bringing

37

the scent of salt air and seaweed. The furniture here was modern Swedish wood, light coloured and comfortable. There was a low divan bed, a dressing table, fitted wardrobes against the curved outer wall, and an easy chair. Orange drapes hung at the windows, and the colour was repeated in the heavy embroidered silk bedspread.

Toni clasped her hands. 'I – er – it's marvellous!' she exclaimed, looking warmly at Luisa. 'It's just perfect!'

Luisa looked pleased. She crossed the room to a door at the far side, and opening it, said: 'Here is the bathroom. Now, I think you have everything here you need. José will bring your cases, and if you require them to be unpacked—'

'That won't be necessary,' replied Toni quickly, remembering that there might be some identification in her suitcases. 'Thank you. Oh, by the way, where do I go when I want to go down? I mean, do I go back to the hall?'

Luisa shook her head. 'No, *senhorita*. Instead of turning for the hall, turn the other way and you will come to a small staircase which leads down to the main rooms of the *castelo*. You understand, the *castelo* is too big for the family to occupy all the rooms. Most are dust-covered and locked, *senhorita*. If you follow my directions, the Senhor will find you, yes?'

'Thank you,' Toni smiled, and Luisa withdrew. After she had gone, Toni explored her domain further. From her windows she had an uninterrupted view of the shoreline, the rocky coast which hugged the waters f the Atlantic in its narrow coves and bays.

Then she left the window with a brief sigh, and looked
to the bathroom. It was satisfactorily modern, and
e smiled. She had never had a bathroom all to herself
efore.

A tap at her door heralded the arrival of José with
er cases. She thanked him and after he had gone
et about unpacking. It did not take long and afterwards she looked at her watch. It was a little after six,
ime for a bath before changing for dinner. She stripped
ff her travelling clothes, and studied her reflection in
he long mirror of the wardrobe. She saw a tall, slim
irl, with firmly rounded breasts and hips, and long
lender legs. She knew she was attractive, and yet she
could never understand that anyone could find her
beautiful. Looks could be quite a drawback, she thought
gloomily, remembering Miguel de Calle, and the boy
from the *restaurante*. Then with a resigned sigh, she
went for her bath. Afterwards, she dressed in a tunic of
navy tricel, with a wide white Puritan type of collar,
which was belied by the shortness of its skirt. She wound
her hair on to the top of her head in a Grecian knot,
and studied her appearance again. Did she look too
modern, too careless to be the kind of girl Paul's grandmother would wish him to marry? Well, she would
have to take her as she found her. After all, this was
Paul's idea, and so long as he was satisfied, that should
be all that mattered.

She left her bedroom before she could criticize herself
still further. She followed the corridor back to the main
one, and turned left instead of right, as Luisa had told

her. Then she looked for the small staircase. Whether it was the atmosphere of the place, or just her own nerves, she didn't know, but she had the awful feeling that she had taken a wrong turning somewhere. She seemed to be getting nowhere, and she had an uncomfortable apprehensiveness of meeting a ghost or some-other strange being. She felt rather like Alice in Wonderland, and she wished she could meet somebody, some human, anybody!

Eventually, she stopped and looked back. She had not missed a turning, she couldn't have done. Maybe she had turned the wrong way in the beginning. Maybe she was in that part of the *castelo* that was unoccupied. What had Luisa said: *dust-covered and locked.* It was an eerie thought. But Toni refused to be panicked into shouting for help. Instead, she determinedly crossed to the nearest door and turned the handle briskly, peering into the room.

She saw a huge fourposter bed, illuminated by concealed lighting above the corniced walls; the bed was hung with tasselled bedcovers, from a central device which she realized provided a complete screen when let down; there was an enormous dressing table and wardrobe, but when a figure detached itself from a wickerwork bedroom chair, Toni gave an involuntary gasp of surprise.

'*Boa noite, senhorita. Muito prazer em a ver. Entrar. Seja benvindo!*'

Toni stifled an exclamation, and cautiously moved round the door. 'I – I'm afraid I don't speak much Portuguese, *senhora*,' she murmured awkwardly.

The old lady smiled. 'Ah, you must be Senhorita West, my grandson's fiancée.' Now she spoke in English.

'Oh, Condessa!' Toni swallowed hard. What had she done? 'I'm sorry to intrude! Yes, I'm – I'm Janet West!'

The old lady came forward, shaking her head, and reaching for Toni's hand. 'You do not intrude, my dear. I am glad of this opportunity to speak with you, without all the preliminaries of introduction, and so on. But I would like to know, are you lost? Or did you come to find me?'

'I'm afraid I was looking for a staircase, leading down to the apartments which are in use. I was afraid I was in the part of the *castelo* which is unused. I thought if I looked into a room . . .' Her voice trailed away, and she linked her fingers together nervously. What a ghastly thing to have happened! To be confronted by the one person she was here to impress, without Paul's reassuring presence!

But the Dowager Condessa della Maria Estrada did not strike Toni as being a particularly frightening person, and certainly not the martinet that Paul had made her out to be if she was any judge. Unless she was completely mistaken, which she supposed was possible.

'Did you have a good journey?' the old lady was asking, indicating that she should be seated.

Toni perched on the edge of the chair, looking about the Condessa's apartments with interest. Here was evidence of the old *castelo* again, no modern furnishings for the Condessa; she obviously liked old things.

'I am almost ready to go down myself,' went on Paul's

grandmother. 'I rest during the afternoons, so I was not there to greet you on your arrival. You must have thought us very uncharitable.'

'Oh, no! That is – Paul's cousin met us. Francesca.'

'Ah, Francesca. And what did you think of her, *senhorita?*'

Toni didn't know what she was expected to answer. She felt sure the Condessa would see through any subterfuge she might adopt. 'She – well, she seems a rather lonely child.'

The Condessa smiled, switching on a standard lamp and by so doing adding a golden glow to the rich texture of the polished wood. 'I can tell from your discomfiture you thought Francesca rude and unwelcoming!' she said candidly.

Toni flushed. 'Oh, I – no, Condessa. I'm sure I didn't mean to give that impression—'

'Do not be alarmed, *senhorita* – or may I call you Janet?' Toni nodded, and she continued: 'Francesca is rather a problem child, my dear. Her mother was killed when she was only three years old, and I am afraid my son does not spend as much time with her as perhaps he should. He spends much of his time in Lisbon, burying himself in his work. He has little time for her and consequently I spoil her utterly.' She shrugged. 'It is difficult. The child had a governess, but Mademoiselle was less than useless, so we had to get rid of her. Now she is left to run wild, with this result!'

'I see.' Toni inclined her head. 'Would it not be better to get someone else to care for her, someone who could handle her?'

'No doubt it would. But who? My dear, we are quite isolated here and young people want the life of the cities these days.' She sighed. 'To Raoul she is without fault, and indeed, when he is around, her behaviour much improves.'

Toni wondered. She thought Francesca's father was blind to his daughter's shortcomings. As he saw her so little, the child would grow up thinking herself perfect in his eyes, which was always bad for the child anyway. With her interest in children, Toni thought it would be hard not to voice her opinions.

'Tell me a little about yourself,' said the Condessa now. 'I understand you work for the same company as Paul.'

Toni concentrated hard. 'Yes. I – I work in the typing pool.'

'Have you known Paul long?'

That was more difficult; she had never asked him that question. 'Long enough,' she prevaricated, with a forced laugh, glad to see that the old lady did not consider her reply in any way extraordinary.

'And when are you planning to get married?' Then, suddenly: 'My dear, where is your ring?'

A ring! Toni felt her cheeks burning. They hadn't discussed that either. 'My – my ring,' she said. 'I – er – it was too big, so it's being made smaller. We couldn't bring it with us.'

'Oh,' the Condessa relaxed. 'I thought perhaps you had lost it. It is very unlucky to lose one's betrothal ring.'

'Oh, I haven't lost it,' said Toni, with some confidence. That, at least, was the truth.

'And you didn't tell me when you're planning to get married.'

Toni swallowed hard. 'No. I – er – I suppose we're saving up as fast as we can, but I'm sure you realize everything is so expensive. . . .' Her voice trailed away, and she prayed this would satisfy the Condessa.

The Condessa smiled a little conspiratorially. 'But of course, my dear, the expense of it all! Still, as I'm sure Paul has told you, I am going to see that your finances are considerably improved before you leave here.'

'What!' Toni stared at her in astonishment. Then, twisting her hands awkwardly, she said: 'Paul didn't – say much about it!' falteringly. Inwardly, she seethed. What was all this about? And what did the Condessa mean about improving Paul's finances? Was this why Paul had been so urgently desirous of a fiancée? Her thoughts raced. She had had her suspicions of Paul earlier, but she had not thought to have her doubts crystallized within a couple of hours of setting foot in the *castelo*.

Happily, the Condessa dropped this topic of conversation and reverted back to their journey and Toni's first impressions of Portugal. In this Toni could be completely truthful; she told the Condessa she already loved the country, and was sure she was going to enjoy her stay enormously.

An elderly servant appeared whom the Condessa addressed as Elena and she proceeded to comb the old lady's hair, and help her to choose some jewellery from a box on the dressing table. Even to Toni's inexperienced young eyes the gems sparkling and glinting in their satin-lined case looked to be worth a small fortune, and she moved uncomfortably, unused to the evidence of such wealth, and not particularly liking it.

Then the Condessa said she was ready, and taking Toni's arm, she said: 'Come, Janet, we will go down to meet my grandson together.'

The staircase Toni had been searching for lay around a bend in the corridor, and they descended together to a small chandelier-hung hallway, where Paul was waiting for them, looking tall and handsome in dark dinner clothes. He stared in astonishment at Toni with his grandmother, and his eyes darted to Toni's with something questioning in their depths. Toni gave an infinitesimal shake of her head, and he seemed to visibly relax.

He greeted his grandmother warmly, kissing her on both cheeks, and she smiled rather roguishly at him. 'I have already met your charming fiancée, Paul,' she said, allowing him to link her arm with his. 'We met by accident, but I am sure it has proved more enjoyable for both of us than formal greetings could ever be, don't you agree, Janet?'

Toni managed to nod casually, a smile on her face, while inwardly she longed to speak to Paul and confront him with her acquired knowledge.

Paul, oblivious of any undercurrents, was delighted. 'I knew you two would take to one another,' he enthused. 'Janet – likes all this kind of thing, old buildings and historical places.'

Toni wanted to deny the things Paul was saying

45

despite their truth. He was using her genuine interest to capitalize on it.

'Paul's a modernist,' she said coolly, ignoring his annoyed expression at her words. 'He likes to spend money, not look at it. In something of such monumental interest as this castle he can only see the monetary value!'

Paul flushed. 'To— Janet's joking, of course,' he said sharply, and Toni trembled a little at the slip he almost made. 'Naturally, she likes to tease me!'

The Condessa appeared not a wit concerned by this exchange, and smiled benevolently. 'Oh, you young people,' she said. 'How you like to bicker between yourselves! In my day, a girl would not dare to answer back her fiancée, Janet. You don't appreciate the freedom you have, my dear.'

Toni gave a wry smile, and then followed them across the hall into a long, high-ceilinged room where on a polished refectory table dinner was being served. Exquisitely embroidered place mats were set with silver cutlery, while every place had a selection of wine glasses in cut crystal. A centre piece of magnolias and roses complemented the silver candelabra, real candles burning in their sconces. Toni could not control the gasp of pleasure that escaped her, and the Condessa smiled in a satisfied way, and indicated that she should be seated. The Condessa sat at the head of the table with Paul on her right and Toni on her left. Then she beckoned the servant.

'Will you tell Senhorita Francesca we are waiting for her,' she said imperiously.

The servant bowed low. 'Senhorita Francesca has asked for dinner to be served in her room,' he said, politely, in English.

'Tell the Senhorita Francesca that we are waiting for her,' replied the Condessa coldly. 'Tell her to come *at once!*'

'*Sim, senhora.*' The manservant withdrew, and a few silent, uncomfortable minutes later a petulant Francesca appeared in the doorway, still dressed in the skirt and blouse she had been wearing that afternoon.

'Sit down, Francesca,' said her grandmother smoothly, and then when the girl did so with ill grace, the Condessa indicated that the servants should begin serving the meal.

Toni thought that the Condessa had more about her than she had at first imagined, and yet there was gentleness behind the request, and Francesca had responded to it without question.

The meal progressed in silence for a while, until the Condessa began speaking to Paul about his parents, and how his job was faring. Toni barely listened to their comments. She was intensely aware of Francesca, and her emotions, which were almost tangible things. Even the *lagosta suada a moda de peniche*, which was a delicious dish of lobster and olives in a wine sauce, could not dispel the arrogant dislike emanating from the younger girl on her left.

When the meal was over, they adjourned to a small lounge, and liqueurs were served with aromatic continental coffee. After her grandmother and Paul and Toni were seated, Francesca said:

'Will you excuse me now, Avó?'

The Condessa looked up at her coldly. 'No, indeed not, Francesca. You will sit down with Janet and speak with her while I talk to Paul.'

'Oh, really—' began Toni awkwardly.

'Do not be uncomfortable, my dear,' said the Condessa, smiling firmly. 'Francesca must make amends for her tardy behaviour this afternoon. Agreed, *neta*?'

Francesca looked sulky, but she subsided on to the low couch beside Toni and said: 'Very well, Avó.'

Toni accepted a cigarette from Paul, and after it was lit, she looked at Francesca thoughtfully. 'Tell me, Francesca,' she said, 'do *you* like it here, at Estrada?'

Francesca shrugged, and then catching her grandmother's warning eye, answered: 'Yes, I love it, *senhorita*.'

'Francesca,' said the Condessa, 'it is not necessary to call your cousin's fiancée *senhorita*. You may address her as Janet, as she is soon to be one of the family.'

Toni flushed anew, and at last aroused Francesca's curiosity. 'Do *you* like it here?' she countered. 'After all, I do not suppose you are accustomed to staying in castles.' The words were deliberately rude, but Toni chose to ignore the fact.

'No,' she said easily, in reply, 'I am not used to staying in castles, as you point out. However, I expect I shall learn.'

Francesca scowled. 'Do you expect to stay long?'

Toni shrugged. 'Long enough to teach an ignorant teenager some manners, perhaps,' she remarked casually.

'You see, I am learning already. Are these perhaps the conversations of people who live in castles these days?'

Francesca looked absolutely flabbergasted. She stared at Toni now, and caught the mocking twinkle in Toni's eyes. Unwillingly a faint smile touched Francesca's lips, and then she stifled it as though ashamed of her own sense of humour.

'Now,' said Toni equably, 'perhaps we can have some intelligent conversation without this constant antagonism.'

Francesca shrugged. 'What about?'

'Tell me about the bathing here. Is it good?'

'Yes,' said Francesca slowly. 'Below the *castelo* there is a rock basin which is perfect for swimming when the tide is right. The water is never cold, as it is in England.'

'You know England?' said Toni with interest.

'I have been there, with my father. We stayed in London for a while, and then we went to a place on your south coast called – what is it? – Bourne – Bourne—' She shook her head.

'Bournemouth?' Toni supplied.

'Yes, Bournemouth. It is a nice place, but the water is cold.'

'We do not get the sun in England as you do here,' Toni reminded her. 'And the waters of the English Channel are not the warm waters of the Portuguese Atlantic.'

'That I found, to my cost.' Francesca shivered. 'But my father likes England, so I suppose one day we will go again. He visits London often in the course of his business, but I am not allowed to accompany him.' She sounded dejected, and for a moment Toni felt sorry for her.

'Did you see Buckingham Palace, when you were in London?'

Francesca was at last enthusiastic. 'Oh, yes, and the Tower of London, and Hampton Court. We were just ordinary tourists. It was wonderful!'

Toni smiled in agreement, and then Francesca, as though becoming aware that she was being too expansive, became silent again, and Toni gave up trying to talk to her. It was obvious that Francesca was not going to be an easy person to get to know, but it was possible to break the shell if one tried hard enough, and with the right ammunition.

The rest of the evening passed pleasantly enough. Francesca was excused later, and after Toni had given up trying to speak to Paul for a moment alone, she too excused herself and retired to her bedroom. Whether Paul was aware of her desire to speak with him or not she was uncertain, but one thing was certain, and that was Paul's less than accurate invitation to join him in pleasing his grandmother. Paul's reasons for producing a fiancée so promptly were all monetary ones, Toni was sure, and she resented being used in this way. She was beginning to wish she had never come.

CHAPTER THREE

THE next morning Toni was awakened by a young maidservant entering her room with a tray containing a glass of fresh orange juice and a small jug of coffee.

'*Bom dia, senhorita,*' she said, smiling, and placing the tray on the table beside the bed.

'*Bom dia.*' Toni struggled into a sitting position, brushing back the swathe of heavy hair that fell forward as she did so. 'What time is it?'

'*Desculpe-me, senhorita?*' The girl looked puzzled, and Toni gave a smiling shake of her head indicating that it was not important, and with a brief bob the maid left the room. Obviously she did not understand English, and Toni thought she would have to get a Portuguese phrase book if she wanted to make herself understood.

The fruit juice and coffee were delicious. Toni sipped her coffee as she crossed the room barefooted to swing wide her windows and gaze out disbelievingly at the fantastic view that awaited her. The sea was breaking in iridescent foam on the greenish-grey rocks, while a pale sun was filtering through a faint cloud formation. The sand looked almost white, and Toni longed to put on her bathing suit and go for a swim. But until she knew a little more about the habits of the household she did not like to presume too much.

However, as she watched, she saw a figure appear

from a small door set in the stone wall of the castle. Recognizing it as Francesca Toni watched as the girl found a pathway round the rim of the moat until she came to a small footbridge. She was carrying a string bag, and Toni saw her cross the grass to the side of the castle that swept down to the cliffs above the beach. She disappeared down a path near the cliffs and Toni thought she must have gone swimming. Her suspicions were confirmed a few minutes later when Francesca reappeared on the beach, and began shedding a loose robe she was wearing over her bathing suit. Toni sighed. She wished Francesca had mentioned swimming last evening. After all, the child must be lonely doing everything by herself.

Eventually she withdrew, ran herself a bath, and after bathing dressed in slim-fitting green pants, and a sleeveless green overblouse made of *broderie anglaise*. She looked cool and attractive, her long hair gathered into two bunches with elastic bands.

She descended the staircase she and the Condessa had used the night before and entered the dining-room. There was no one about, but in a few minutes another maid came to ask her what she would like for breakfast. This maid spoke broken English, and Toni was grateful. She explained that all she wanted was some coffee and rolls, and then wandered about the room exploring until it arrived. Half-way through her meal, Francesca appeared, her plait soaked and untidy, dressed in the same skirt and blouse she had worn the day before. Really, thought Toni, to remember Francesca was the daughter of a man who owned a castle was difficult when she continually dressed as though she had nothing else.

After wishing the child '*Bom dia*,' and receiving no reply but an insolent stare, Toni felt her temper rising. Controlling it with difficulty, she said: 'I wish you had told me you were going swimming, Francesca. I would like to have gone with you.'

Francesca stared at her. 'Why should you?'

Toni sighed. 'Well, why do you suppose? I like swimming. Is that answer enough for you?'

Francesca shrugged. 'Paul never gets up before noon when he's here, and my grandmother is the same. Maybe it would be as well if you acted likewise.'

Toni looked down at her coffee. 'Why are you so objectionable, Francesca?' she asked coolly.

Francesca was obviously taken aback. 'I don't know what you mean,' she said sulkily.

'Yes, you do. You know perfectly well what I mean. I would like to know, though, what have I done to deserve such treatment? Heavens, we only met yesterday!'

'You're Paul's fiancée,' said Francesca.

'So what! I know you don't like Paul, he told me so, but there's no reason for you to dislike me, surely?'

Francesca buttered a roll, and bit it thoughtfully. 'Why has Paul come here?' she asked.

Toni felt hot, but managed to control her blushes. She had no intention of allowing Francesca to see she had embarrassed her. 'To see his grandmother,' she replied.

Francesca snorted. 'Some hopes! Paul only comes

here when he wants money. If you thought he came to see Avó you're more gullible than I thought!'

'Don't be impertinent,' said Toni, frowning. 'Even were anything of that sort true, which I am sure it's not, you're far too young to be making comments about it. It's nothing to do with you.' She finished her coffee. 'I think you're jealous, that's all. But why you should be jealous of me—'

Francesca laughed. 'I'm not jealous of *you*,' she said, and the way she said it was in itself insolence.

Toni rose from the table, reaching for her cigarettes and lighting one. Francesca watched her.

'Papa won't approve of you wearing slacks,' she said, with some satisfaction.

Toni gave her an exasperated look. 'Really! Is that so? I'm positively quaking in my shoes!'

Francesca looked mutinous and returned her attention to her rolls and butter. Without waiting for her to finish Toni left the room. She wasn't sure where she was going, but she had no intention of allowing Senhorita Francesca della Maria Estrada to arouse her any longer. The hall offered a selection of doors and Toni chose one. A corridor led to yet another door, and feeling quite adventurous now, Toni followed it, feeling quite disappointed when it opened into the courtyard that they had driven into the previous afternoon. She had thought she might find something exciting. However, deciding she might as well explore as wait around for Paul to get up, she ventured forward. Obviously Francesca knew Paul's habits better than she did.

She spent the morning on the beach. Following the path she had seen Francesca take, she found the steps hewn out of the cliff face which led down to the sandy cove. She rolled up her slacks and paddled, then searched for shells among the rocks as she had done as a child. The sun was warm on her shoulders, and the sense of well-being returned. Only Francesca's antagonism prevented her from feeling completely happy.

She returned in good time for lunch, carrying her sandals in her hand. Entering the courtyard, she was surprised to see a low grey limousine in the parking area. Visitors already? She entered the house by way of the small passage and emerged into the hall. Hearing sounds from the lounge, she walked towards its entrance, wondering if she could see Paul alone now. The lounge was a modern room in most respects, with a stereo-radiogram and a television set, as well as a small cocktail bar. But it was deserted apart from Eduardo, the manservant, who had attended them at dinner the previous evening. He was busy at the cocktail bar, mixing a drink, but as though aware of her presence, he turned, and said: '*Sim, senhorita?*'

Toni smiled and shook her head disappointedly. 'It was nothing, Eduardo,' she said. 'I was looking for Senhor Paul.'

'*Com efeito, senhorita, senão porque?*' said a voice behind her.

Toni gasped and swung round to confront a man standing in the doorway, a tall dark man, with a thin livid scar marring the tanned flesh of his cheek. 'You!' she exclaimed, before she could prevent herself. It was the man who had almost knocked her down in Lisbon.

He gave a slight bow of recognition, but his eyes narrowed. 'Why are you here in my house?' he asked in a cool voice, speaking English now.

Toni swallowed hard. 'Your house?' she echoed faintly.

'Yes, *senhorita*, my house.'

'Then you are. . . .' Her voice trailed away.

'The Conde Raoul Felipe Vincente della Maria Estrada, *senhorita*!' He said the words with arrogant emphasis, and Toni shook her head nervously. This man, this tall, lean, arrogant Portuguese, was Paul's uncle, and Francesca's father! Dressed today in a cream lounge suit, his thick hair lying smoothly against his well-shaped head, he was equally as disturbing as that day in Lisbon, and for a few moments Toni found it difficult to gather her scattered wits. She thought back wildly, trying to remember whether she had revealed her name to him and then giving an involuntary shake of her head. Even so. . . .

'I repeat, why are you in my house?' he said, his voice cold.

Toni wondered hysterically for a moment whether he thought she had traced him in order to try and extract some kind of retribution from him for her near accident, but seeing the sombre expression on his face she thrust these thoughts aside.

'I – er – your nephew Paul brought me,' she stammered awkwardly.

'He did!' His expression hardened still further. 'Why?'

Toni was self-consciously aware of her bare feet, of her close-fitting slacks, which Francesca had said her father would not approve of, of her bare arms and tangled hair, and most of all of her own insignificance. Her five feet six inches had always seemed to place her on eye-level terms with the men of her acquaintance, but as the Conde della Maria Estrada was easily six feet in height, he seemed to tower over her like some avenging angel. In consequence, she felt immediately at a disadvantage.

'Paul – is – my fiancé,' she said, at last.

The old manservant Eduardo gave a slight cough, and the Conde looked beyond Toni to the old man. '*Esta bem*, Eduardo?'

'*Sim, senhor.*'

'*Muito obrigado*, Eduardo!'

The manservant, smiled, bowed, and withdrew, but when Toni would have followed him, the Conde said:

'A moment, *senhorita*.'

Toni swallowed hard. Was she destined to face all these interviews with Paul's family alone? This was the second time due to her curiosity she had landed herself in a difficult situation.

'Yes, *senhor*,' she said resignedly, determinedly ignoring the shaky feeling he aroused in the pit of her stomach. She had never met anyone who remotely resembled this man, and until now she had thought she knew most everything there was to know about sexual attraction. Which was in itself ridiculous really. After all, the Conde was considerably older than she was, and from the slightly jaded expression he wore she

57

thought not only in actual age but in experience, too. He was surveying her with a rather cynical glint in his dark eyes, and she moved uncomfortably, wishing he would stop looking at her. There was a kind of insolence about his gaze which was not unlike the kind of glances Francesca had given her. She felt her temper rising at this realization. What right had he to treat her so carelessly?

'Senhor,' she said, breaking the uneasy silence which had fallen, 'will you please tell me what it is you have to say and let me go!'

'Patience,' replied the Conde sardonically, and turning away approached the cocktail bar where Eduardo had left a shaker full of liquid and a crystal glass waiting for him.

Toni contemplated ignoring him altogether and leaving the room, but that would be very rude, and she was not used to behaving in such a manner. On the other hand, she was not used to this kind of sustained battle of nerves, and she wished there was a chair nearby, for she was afraid her legs might not remain firm. She had already had one sample of the kind of anger the Conde possessed that day in Lisbon, and she had no wish to arouse him again, as much for her own sake as Paul's.

The Conde poured two drinks, extracting a glass from below the serving surface. Then he added two squares of ice to each, and turning came across and handed one to Toni.

Then he passed her, closed the lounge door with a firm click, and came back to her. Toni did not touch her drink.

The Conde swallowed half of his, and then said: 'The drink is not to your liking, *senhorita*?'

Toni compressed her lips for a moment. 'I don't drink at this hour of the day, Senhor Conde.'

He looked amused. 'Do you not, *senhorita*? Why?'

Toni was speechless. Why didn't she? Should she explain that in the social sphere she moved in drinks were not a natural accompaniment to living? Instead, she said: 'I do not drink very much at all, Senhor Conde.'

He smiled sarcastically. 'Then you are indeed unique in Paul's small circle of friends,' he said, shrugging his broad shoulders. Toni noticed the movement. Although his shoulders were broad, his hips were narrow, and there was not an ounce of spare flesh on his body. Her eyes were drawn to his scar, and she wondered how it came to be there, then flushed as she realized she was staring. 'Does this—' he flicked a hand at his scar '—does this disturb you?' His eyes narrowed. 'I have grown so used to living with it I forget its appearance can offend people.'

Toni shook her head. 'No, it does not disturb me, Senhor Conde,' she replied, bending her head.

He seemed sceptical of her reply. In any event, he moved further away from her, turning so that side of his face was hidden. 'So, *senhorita*,' he went on, 'you are Paul's fiancée. That is very interesting. Can you then tell me what you were doing wandering alone about the streets of Lisbon, in apparent need of an escort?'

Toni flushed, again. 'Paul – Paul was – he was

59

making arrangements for hiring the car to bring us here,' she finished quickly.

'I see.' He finished his drink, and crossing to the cocktail bar poured himself another. Then he faced her again. 'No doubt, as you are Paul's fiancée, you are aware of his reasons for bringing you here.'

Toni stiffened. 'What reasons, *senhor*?'

'Come now, I do not believe Paul has not revealed his motives for coming here to you.'

Toni bit her lip. 'Senhor Conde, it is almost lunch time and I wish to change before then. Surely this catechism should be addressed to Paul, not to myself.'

He felt in his pocket and produced a slim gold cigarette case. He extracted a cigarette without offering her one, and after it was lit, he said: 'On the contrary, I think it is necessary that I make the position clear to you.'

Toni, despite her nervousness, was longing for a cigarette, and was rapidly losing patience. 'What position?' She omitted to give him his title, and if he noticed it he made no demur.

'This, *senhorita*,' he said icily. 'That my mother is an old woman, with an old woman's fancies. At the moment, she is of the opinion that Paul is her – how shall I put it? – blue-eyed boy, that is the expression you use, is it not? But I control this estate, and my mother's finances, and I do not intend that she should throw money away on a lazy idiot such as Paul Craig!'

Toni's eyes were wide and indignant. Whatever Paul had done this uncle of his had no right to speak of him so contemptuously.

'What has this to do with me?' she asked angrily.

He gave a short mirthless laugh. 'Oh, really, *senhorita*, surely I do not have to tell you that! If your intention to marry my nephew has any basis on his expectations from his grandmother, then I am afraid you are going to be sadly disappointed!'

'How dare you!' Toni stared at him furiously. He was so cool and calm and assured, and there was absolutely nothing she could do about it.

'Oh, you will find I dare a lot of things,' he replied indolently. 'Not least being the authority to call black black, and not a dirty shade of grey.'

Toni stepped forward, she had never felt so angry, or so impotent, and she longed to strike that sardonic expression from his lean face. She was on the point of raising her hand, when steel-hard fingers closed round her wrist, preventing the action before it was actually motivated. 'I think not,' he murmured, looking down at her with brilliantly mocking eyes.

'Papa!' The young voice was as unexpected as a cold shower, and as cooling. Immediately, Toni was free, rubbing her sore wrist where his hard fingers had hurt her, looking round at the puzzled, angry face of the girl who was standing just inside the door. 'Papa,' she said, more slowly, looking at Toni with blazing eyes, then continuing to speak in their own language so that Toni was completely excluded from the conversation.

With a muffled exclamation, Toni brushed past them, uncaring then of what Francesca might think, and with legs that were none too steady she ran up the stairs to the sanctuary of her room.

CHAPTER FOUR

TONI didn't know how she was going to summon up enough courage to go downstairs for lunch. Surveying herself later in her bedroom with her face flushed and stained with hot, angry tears and her hair an untidy mess, she found her indignation giving way to a trembling awareness of something that bordered on hatred that would listen to no defence. No wonder Paul had refrained from telling her his real reasons for bringing her to Estrada. How could he have revealed such a situation? She doubted whether Janet would have agreed to come had she known the truth.

She gave a heavy sigh. There was only one thing to do, of course. She must see Paul, it was imperative now, and explain that she wanted to leave immediately. She would not stay here to be insulted again by either the Conde or his daughter. This decision made, she felt a little better, and could not understand the faint feeling of regret she was experiencing at the knowledge she was soon to bid the *castelo* farewell. It could only be that she would not enjoy disappointing the old Condessa who had treated her so kindly.

Eventually she washed, combed her hair into a knot on top of her head, and dressed in a semi-flared blue skirt and navy shirt blouse. The skirt was the shortest in her wardrobe, and she wore it deliberately. At least the Conde should not have the satisfaction of seeing that she was afraid of him.

She descended the stairs, ignoring the jelly-like feeling in her legs with difficulty, and entered the lounge rather apprehensively. To her relief only Paul was there standing by the bar drinking a glass of wine appreciatively. He was smoking a long continental cigarette which he waved at her languidly. 'Hi, Janet,' he said. 'This wine can be really enjoyable, you know!'

'Paul, I want to talk to you,' she said without preamble.

He shrugged his shoulders. 'Do you? Say, I like that outfit. Makes you look really something!'

Toni gave him an exasperated look. 'Paul, this is serious. I want to leave here today, at once!'

Paul's expression changed from one of lazy indolence to disturbed irritation. 'Why? What has Francesca said now? I'll tan her hide when I get my hands on her!'

'Not Francesca,' said Toni, shaking her head. 'I can handle Francesca. Are you aware that your Uncle Raoul is here?'

Paul started. 'Raoul!' he echoed.

'Yes, the Conde.' Toni linked her fingers. 'Oh, give me a cigarette. Believe me, I need one. And you – you are the biggest liar I know!'

Paul looked uncomfortable. 'What do you mean?'

'You know damn nicely what I mean,' exclaimed Toni, leaning forward to light her cigarette from the lighter he proffered. 'Before dinner last evening I learned the reason why you were in such a hurry to arrive here with a fiancée.'

'Wnat!'

'Yes; now say it isn't money! That is the reason, isn't it? Oh, don't bother to deny it. I can tell from your face that I'm right. Honestly, what do you think I am?'

Paul looked a little shamefaced. 'I don't see why you're getting so het up about it,' he muttered sulkily. 'It doesn't make any difference to you. You're still having a free holiday, and my reasons are my own and no one else's.'

Toni's eyes blazed. 'You're a positive menace, Paul,' she stormed angrily. 'You've succeeded in getting me into *the* most awful situation of my life!'

Paul frowned. 'Why? What did my grandmother say?'

'Oh, not your *grandmother*,' cried Toni, shaking her head. 'Your uncle! He seems to consider me some kind of gold-digger who has come here with you to try and inveigle some money out of his mother! When he spoke to me in here earlier on – well, I felt so big!' She put her first finger and thumb close together. 'Not that I consider his opinion of me so important, but I do not intend to put up with that kind of treatment any longer. I'm leaving! You can please yourself whether you follow my example!'

'Toni!'

'Well!' Toni walked about restlessly, smoking nervously. 'You must be out of your tiny mind if you think your grandmother is going to help you financially with *big brother* looking on!'

Paul stubbed out his own cigarette. 'My grandmother has money of her own,' he said stiffly. 'What she does with it is her own concern. Besides, you don't know the whole story. My mother has never had a penny from this family. They've never lifted a finger to help her! Why should I care if my motives for coming here are misconstrued? In a way, I'm paying them back for the way they treated my mother.'

'And how long do you imagine you're going to be allowed to get away with it, with Uncle Raoul watching your every move like a hawk?'

'My grandmother doesn't require his permission for the things she does,' retorted Paul exasperatedly. 'Besides, she's still an old woman, who does want to see me married. Even you must have gathered the truth of that.'

'Yes, but that's the point, Paul. This is all pretence! We aren't going to get married!'

Paul studied her thoughtfully. 'We may just do that thing,' he said slowly.

Toni's eyes narrowed. 'Oh, no, Paul. Not me!'

'Why? Am I so repugnant?'

'No. It's not that.' She cast about in her mind for some way to let him down lightly. How could she tell him that he already had assumed a rather weak and indolent stature in her eyes? How also could she explain to herself the instant picture of a tall dark Portuguese who sprang unwanted into her mind at the thought of marriage to another man? 'It's just that we aren't at all alike, and I guess we just don't strike the right sparks off one another.'

Paul moved closer. 'You're beginning to strike the

65

right sparks off me,' he murmured softly. 'Did anyone ever tell you you have the most gorgeous eyes? And your legs. . . .'

'Paul, stop it!' Toni moved jerkily away. 'Don't imagine you can change my mind like that!'

'Why not? All women like flattery.'

'Not all women.'

'Besides, it's not flattery. I mean it. Toni—'

'Stop it, Paul,' she interrupted him. 'What are you going to do?'

'Do? Stay here, of course. How about you?'

Toni stared at him. 'I'm leaving, I've told you.'

'Are you? And have you thought how my dear Uncle Raoul will construe your actions?'

'What do you mean?'

'Well, obviously if he thinks you're a gold-digger, he's going to believe you're leaving because he's found you out. He probably expects you to do just that if you think there's not going to be any money after all.'

Toni ran a hand over her forehead impatiently. Of course, for once Paul had to be right. That was exactly what the arrogant Conde would think. After all, his reasons for informing her of his position were all gauged to produce just such a reaction. He wanted them to leave, particularly Paul, but if Paul had proved to have too thick a skin then obviously the next thing to do was to antagonize his fiancée so badly that she refused to stay and left, more than likely taking the offending Paul with her.

She drew deeply on her cigarette, and Paul, sensing her changing attitude, pressed home his point. 'Do you want Uncle Raoul to get his own way?' he asked. 'I would have thought that anyone with the minutest amount of spunk would give anything for the chance to get back at him, not run and hide like a beaten cat!'

Toni studied the glowing tip of her cigarette, and then when it almost burned her fingers stubbed it out angrily. 'Why should I care what your sainted uncle thinks of me?' she exclaimed.

Paul laughed. 'I don't know. But you do, don't you?' He ran a tongue over his lips. 'Or is it Francesca? After all, if you leave here the laugh will certainly be on us, won't it?'

Toni heaved a sigh. 'I don't like deceiving your grandmother,' she insisted wearily.

'Well, that was the situation long before you left Lisbon,' he reminded her.

'I know, I know! I ought never to have come!'

'I would agree with that,' remarked Conde della Maria Estrada, walking lazily into the room, accompanied by a smirking Francesca.

Toni felt hot angry tears pricking her eyelids suddenly, and she brushed them away with a careless hand, ignoring them all, and walking across to the window. Was she indeed allowing Paul to seduce her into a position where it was impossible for her to retreat? She didn't know. All she did know was that the Conde aroused the strongest feelings inside her, primarily an impotent kind of fury, which longed for satisfaction. He was so cold and aloof, so arrogant and assured. A god on a pedestal, so far as Francesca was concerned. How Toni would love to rock that pedestal a little! It might be foolish pride, but she couldn't stand his indifference.

She swung round to face them all, her mind made up. 'I'm sorry to disappoint you, Senhor Conde,' she said smoothly, realizing anger would gain her nothing. 'But now that I am here, I intend to stay, so long as Paul wants to do so.' She moved across to Paul, and allowed him to place his arm familiarly across her shoulders. 'Isn't that so, *darling*?'

Paul looked down at her, half laughingly, half relieved, and nodded. 'If you say so, honey,' he murmured, and kissed the pink curve of her ear.

The rest of the day passed almost normally. After lunch Toni submitted to the Portuguese habit of siesta, and then in the cool of the later afternoon, she and Paul went out in the hired car, taking the coast road through some beautiful countryside. When they returned it was time to change for dinner, and to Toni's relief she found that the Conde was not present at the dinner table. But the old Condessa was there, and she said:

'I hope you will excuse my son, the Conde, *senhorita*, but he will not be dining with us this evening. He had an engagement with friends. . . .' She smiled gently. 'But I understand from Francesca that you met him at lunch time. I was not present, I am afraid. There are days when I do not feel strong enough to get up so early.'

'I understand, Condessa,' said Toni, smiling in return. Francesca, dressed this evening more formally in a blue velvet shift, gave a knowing, sneering grin. 'The Senhorita perhaps got a little more than she bargained for at lunchtime,' she said insolently.

The Condessa frowned. 'What is that supposed to mean, Francesca?' while Toni gave Paul a helpless glance.

'Senhorita West and my father had a little argument,' replied Francesca, in a smug way.

The Condessa looked at Toni. 'This is so?'

Toni moved awkwardly. 'It was nothing, Condessa. Merely a difference of opinion.'

'Indeed? And perhaps concerning myself?'

Toni gave Francesca an exasperated look. What was she supposed to say now? As though repenting a little, Francesca interposed: 'No, Avó, it was not to do with you.'

The Condessa looked relieved, and Toni looked down at her plate. It seemed that even Francesca had a streak of decency in her when it came to her grandmother.

After dinner, Paul and his grandmother were again esconced together on the long couch in the lounge, but Toni was restless. She looked thoughtfully at Francesca, and said:

'Do you want to go for a walk?'

Francesca looked at her grandmother, saw her expectant expression, and nodded abruptly. Toni collected a cardigan, and they left the castle by the door Toni had used that morning. Once outside the courtyard, Francesca turned away from the beach, and led Toni through the moonlit formal gardens flanking the castle on three sides. Here there were flower gardens, and herbal gardens, rose and vegetable gardens, arbours bright with flowering bougainvillea and dripping with magnolia petals. The sky above them was hung with stars, and even Francesca's uncommunicative presence could not prevent Toni's enjoyment of the night air. The scent of the pine trees was intoxicating, while the roar of the sea was a crescendo in their ears.

They halted in an arbour where a stone seat surrounded a marble fountain which spouted its unending stream of water unceasingly. Toni sat down on the seat, and looked up at Francesca reflectively.

'Why did you do it?' she asked.

Francesca shrugged. 'What?'

'You know – tell your grandmother that the argument I had with your father was not about her.'

Francesca shrugged. 'Whatever else I may do, I do not hurt my grandmother heedlessly,' she replied. 'Do not imagine I did it for you, *senhorita*. I do not care what happens to you!'

Toni sighed. 'I see. Well, thank you anyway. It got me out of an awkward situation, even if you were directly responsible for that situation.'

Francesca allowed her fingers to trail in the waters of the fountain. 'Tell me,' she said, surprisingly, 'do you love Paul?'

Toni was glad the night hid her blushes. 'I – yes, I suppose so.'

Francesca straightened, wiping her hand on the skirt of her dress. 'Aren't you sure?'

'All right, yes, I am.' Toni was irritated.

'Good.' Francesca looked at her piercingly. 'Just don't get any other ideas, will you, *senhorita*?'

'I don't know what you mean!'

'Yes, you do, I mean – my father!'

'What!'

Francesca looked a trifle mocking. 'Don't pretend you don't find him attractive!'

Toni stood up. 'Your mind appals me!' She shook her head. 'It's more devious than a maze!'

'*Mas,*' I am usually right.' Francesca wrinkled her nose. 'But in any case I do not think I have to worry. You are not the type to appeal to my father. He already finds Laura Passamentes more than a distraction.'

Toni pulled out her cigarettes. 'And you don't mind that?' she asked curiously, extracting a cigarette.

'Who? Laura Passamentes? Of course not. My father is of the age where he is too young to remain a widower, and too old to fall in love. Laura Passamentes is herself a widow, with a boy only a little younger than me. If they marry, the situation will be ideal!'

Toni felt nauseated suddenly. To have this thirteen-year-old girl standing here, talking so callously about her father and his needs, his emotional needs moreover, was positively sickening.

Francesca looked scornfully at her. 'You find it distasteful, I can tell,' she said mockingly. 'Why? Are you English so adept at choosing your marriage partner that you cannot countenance a marriage of convenience?'

'I think you talk a lot of rubbish,' retorted Toni, with distaste.

'Well, be warned!' said Francesca with more violence than she had shown so far.

'I don't need the warning,' retorted Toni angrily. 'I'm not interested in your father one tiny bit, and I can't imagine why you should think it's necessary to tell me this. Unless you have your own doubts!'

Francesca gave a scornful laugh. 'Oh, no, *senhorita*, I have no doubts,' she returned impudently.

The next morning Toni woke early again. Looking at her watch, she saw that it was only a little after six-thirty, but she was no longer tired and she refused to lie in bed just thinking of the beautiful day outside, when she could be part of it.

She got up, and rummaging in a drawer produced what she was looking for, a dark blue one-piece bathing suit. There was also a bikini hidden in her suitcase, but she knew they were forbidden on public beaches. Not that the beach below the *castelo* was public, but she did not want to antagonize the Conde still further. She put on the swimsuit, and a dark blue and green towelling beach dress, which barely covered her thighs. Sandals on her feet, and a towel about her neck, she descended the staircase silently, emerging into the courtyard without mishap. She did not know how to reach the door Francesca had used, so instead she walked out through the main entrance and round the castle walls to the stretch of grass which led to the cliff-

The beach appeared deserted, and she went down the steps, revelling in the new-found freedom. The sun was already beginning to warm the cool air, and she felt vigorously healthy. On the sand, she stepped out of her sandals, shed the beach dress and towel, and ran eagerly into the creaming waves. The chill had her gasping, but it was wonderful, and she swam out eagerly, her hair divided into two bunches with the elastic bands soon soaking about her shoulders. After a while she swam back to the beach, and walked up the sand wringing the water out of her hair. She was completely unaware of another presence until the man's shadow fell across her path. She almost jumped out of her skin, and she said coldly:

'Must you continually appear without warning? Like some evil genie out of a bottle!'

He half-smiled, rather mockingly, and said: '*Desculpe, senhorita.*'

She looked at him for a moment, registering everything about him from the close-fitting dark denim trousers he was wearing together with a mustard-coloured knitted nylon shirt, to the mat of dark hairs which was faintly visible above the opened buttons of the shirt. The sleeves were pushed up to his elbows, and a gold watch glinted among the dark hairs of his wrist. Round his neck he had a slender gold chain, suspended from which was a circular medallion. Toni felt the magnetism of his attraction like a living thing around her, and shivering, she turned away, picking up the towel and beginnning to dry herself.

'Did you enjoy your swim?' he asked lazily, propping one foot up on a rock and gazing out to sea for a few moments.

'Yes, thank you.' Toni was short.

He half-smiled again. 'You appear to have done so,' he murmured, surveying her intently.

Toni hastily donned the beach dress. It was not very satisfactory as a covering, but at least it gave her a little more confidence. She was completely unaware that standing there, slim yet curvaceous, in the dark blue swimsuit, her hair tied in the elastic bands, with no make-up to spoil her faintly tanning complexion, she looked little more than Francesca's age.

'What have you come for, *senhor*?' she asked, linking her fingers together.

'Must there be a reason?'

Toni turned away. 'I would think so, *senhor*. I can't believe that overnight your opinion of me has changed so utterly.'

He straightened, thrusting his hands into his trousers pockets. 'You are very terse, *senhorita*. Do not English-women accept a man's presence without question?'

Toni glanced at him. 'No. Not when the man is Conde Raoul Felipe Vincente della Maria Estrada,' she retorted.

'You remembered my name, *senhorita*. That is interesting. And now I have been told yours – by Francesca. Janet West, is it not?'

Toni did not reply. The Conde extracted his cigarette case and opened it. He studied Toni deliberately for a moment, then put a cigarette between his lips and lit it from the combined lighter. Toni turned away. He was just trying to infuriate her, and he was not going to get away with it.

She picked up her towel and sandals, and began to walk up the beach away from him. As before he halted her. '*Senhorita!*'

She sighed and turned. 'What is it?'

'I am giving a small dinner party this evening, for a few friends. Naturally you and Paul will attend as usual. However, I would suggest you tried to show a little less antagonism when you speak to me. I do not care to have to parry your kind of verbal sparring in front of my friends.'

Toni stared at him, her lips pressed together. Then without another word she marched away up the beach. Oh, he was *insufferable*! Absolutely *insufferable*!'

During the late afternoon Paul took Toni into Estrada, the small town a couple of miles down the coast where most of the trade of the district was executed. There was a small market place where one could buy anything from fish to a carved linen chest, while rich rolls of material caught Toni's eye. She stopped to admire the soft velvets and satins and chiffons, wondering who bought such extravagant luxuries in this place. Deciding she might as well have something with which to fill her time, she bought two lengths to make herself two dresses. One was black velvet and the other apricot chiffon, and after buying cottons and zips, and some lining material, she felt well pleased with the results of their expedition.

Then Paul took her down to see the harbour where

the fish was auctioned when the boats came in. The women carried the fish in flat-bottomed baskets on their heads, and Toni winced when she thought of the smell of their hair. Women stood about talking, watching the two strangers with interest. They wore gold rings in their ears and brightly coloured dresses, and Toni thought it was all very picturesque. She half-wished she had brought a camera to record the scene for dull days back in her bed-sitter in London.

Then it was time to return to the *castelo* and Toni thought uneasily of the dinner party ahead of them. She was not looking forward to it at all, and considered crying off with a headache. Despite the fact that the headache was real enough, she would not admit defeat and instead took two aspirins before going for her bath.

Afterwards she studied the contents of her wardrobe with some misgivings. Most of her clothes were very casual, for she had not thought to be attending a formal dinner party with a Portuguese count and his family. However, there was a red embroidered cotton with a roll collar on which were sewn dozens of tiny sequins, and she thought it would do admirably. It had a low back, a short semi-flared skirt, and a close-fitting bodice. She left her long hair loose for a change, and after putting on a little eye make-up and a colourless lipstick she left her room.

She descended the staircase without meeting anyone, and when she reached the small hall she heard the buzz of conversation which exuded from the lounge. She stood for a moment, listening to all the strange voices and panicking a little at the role she was expected to play. Then, with a mental stiffening of her shoulders, she pushed open the door and entered the room.

Her first impression was that the room was filled with people, but as faces distinguished themselves she saw that there were really only four strangers, apart from the Conde and Condessa, Paul and Francesca. There was also a boy of Francesca's age who looked rather pale and thin.

Her second impression was the most disturbing one. All the women wore black or black and white in varying degrees. Her own red dress with its reasonably short skirt stood out like a colour supplement amongst the regular copies of *The Times*, and her face suffused with colour.

As though sensing her embarrassment, the old Condessa came over to her smiling warmly.

'Ah, Janet, my dear child! We were beginning to wonder where you were.'

Toni lifted her shoulders, her silvery hair swinging silkily. 'I apologise, Condessa. I'm afraid I took longer than I expected. I hope I haven't kept you waiting.'

'Only a moment,' replied the Condessa smoothly. 'Come, let me introduce you.'

Toni glanced Paul's way, and he nodded approvingly. Her eyes flickered over the immaculately clad figure of the Conde, pausing only momentarily to register that he was not alone. A small, delicately made woman stood beside him, her fingers lingering caressingly on the expensive material of his dinner jacket. She was looking up at him, completely oblivious of the other members of the company, and he was inclining his head towards her to listen to what she was saying. His eyes met Toni's, and she immediately looked away. He would not see that she was at all affected by his antagonism.

The Condessa was introducing her to a Senhor Vicarra. He was an elderly man, more fitted to be a friend of the Condessa's than her son, but there was a younger couple who were introduced as Senhor and Senhora Primeiro. Senhora Primeiro seemed very friendly and after a servant had provided Toni with a drink Isobel Primeiro said:

'And how are you enjoying your stay in Portugal, *senhorita*?'

Toni gathered her thoughts and smiled. 'Oh, very much, thank you, *senhora*. It's a very beautiful country. Do you live near here, too?'

'Yes, at Cossima, a few miles north of here. You must get Paul to bring you on a visit to our estate some time. We grow flowers, and it can be most interesting.'

'Thank you,' said Toni politely, sipping her martini. 'But I don't think Paul and I will be staying much longer.'

'What!' Paul joined them. 'Honey, of course we're staying for a while. We can't just hurry away almost as soon as we arrive.'

Toni compressed her lips, quelling the retort she wanted to make. 'You're forgetting my job, *darling*,' she said warningly, her voice cold.

The old Condessa smiled roguishly. 'But your job

78

is only important so long as you and Paul are unmarried,' she said. 'And I'm sure Paul is thinking of changing that status in the not so very distant future, eh, Paul?'

Paul smiled too in a smug way that infuriated Toni. 'Naturally, Grandmother, I can hardly wait to make Janet my wife.' He caught her arm possessively. 'She's a beautiful girl, as I'm sure you've noticed.'

Toni longed to wrench her arm out of his grasp. She had never felt so angry or so impotent. He must know he was embarrassing her, and there was an underlying note of truth in his voice that did not go unnoticed.

Another man joined the group accompanied by a small dark woman dressed elegantly in a black silk sheath that moulded her small beautifully proportioned body. Toni was never so glad to see the Conde, although she was well aware of his motives for intervening.

The old Condessa looked dismayed. 'My dear Laura,' she exclaimed, 'how rude you must think me! Of course, you have not yet met our other young guest, Janet. Janet, my dear, this is Senhora Passamentes, a great friend of ours.'

Toni was relieved to release herself from Paul's grasp and go forward to take the other woman's languidly proffered hand. As she did so she looked fully at Laura Passamentes for the first time and felt a faint twinge of recognition. She frowned, as she became aware that Laura was looking at her strangely too, and then the moment was over and she forgot about it.

'How do you do?' said Laura politely.

Toni determined to make an effort to be friendly. 'I'm fine, thank you. The boy with Francesca – is he your son, *senhora*?'

Laura's eyes flickered. 'Yes, that is Estevan, *senhorita*.' Then she looked up at Raoul della Maria Estrada, as though bored by the encounter.

Toni became aware of the interested speculation of the rest of the group, and decided she was not going to get anywhere with this kind of conversation. She glanced at the Conde almost compulsively, seeing the half-mocking lift to his mouth, and felt furiously angry. Obviously, he had taken pains to inform Laura Passamentes of his own feelings towards his nephew's fiancée. As other members of the party began to speak again, Paul joined her.

'Heavy going, isn't it?' he remarked laughingly. 'I shouldn't attempt to catechize the Senhora. She and the Conde are like that.' He twisted his two forefingers together. 'I guess she doesn't like me either.'

Toni shrugged her slim shoulders and gave him a cold glance. 'You yourself don't exactly pull your punches, do you? How dare you make such blatant comments about our marriage!'

'Ssh!' Paul glanced round apprehensively. 'You know perfectly well that I have to behave like that.'

Toni looked sceptical. 'I'm beginning to think you really intend getting me into a situation where there is no retreat.'

'Aw, come on, Ton – Janet!' He flushed annoyedly. 'Look, let's keep these kind of arguments for when we're alone!'

Toni finished her drink and accepted another. She felt a kind of awful fatalism overtake her, and determinedly swallowed the martini in one gulp, ridding herself temporarily of her feelings of guilt and unease.

'Steady on,' exclaimed Paul, in a low angry tone, as his uncle paused beside them. The Conde studied Toni deliberately for a moment.

'So, *senhorita*,' he murmured lazily, 'you do not drink.'

Toni stared at him, then said: 'Give me a cigarette, Paul.'

Paul brought out his cigarettes with angry, jerky movements, but Toni didn't particularly care if she was annoying him. Then to her relief a manservant appeared to inform them that dinner was now ready.

The long table was fully occupied this evening, and Toni found herself between Paul and Estevan Passamentes. The boy seemed more friendly than his mother, and Toni found herself talking to him quite naturally. His English was very good, and she ignored Francesca, who was glowering at her from Estevan's other side. Paul seemed sullen and withdrawn, and she could only assume she had succeeded in arousing his real anger this time.

When the meal was over, they adjourned to the lounge again, and Laura Passamentes was prevailed upon to entertain them. Toni, sitting on a low couch beside Isabel Primeiro, wondered how Laura was going to do this. Estevan was despatched from the room, and returned a moment later carrying a guitar case from which Laura took a beautifully polished instrument. It seemed obvious that her assumed reluctance to agree to the Conde's suggestion had merely been a kind of pretence.

However, when she started to sing, Toni's objections died away, as Laura's pure clear voice sang some of the folk music of her country. The music was gay and colourful, and her audience responded warmly when she finished her song. Isabel looked at Toni rather thoughtfully:

'What do you think of our culture, Senhorita West? Do you like this kind of emotional expression?'

Toni smiled. 'Oh, yes, very much. I think the folk music of a country epitomizes all this is basic and fundamental in its people.'

'Yes, I would agree,' said Georges Primeiro. 'Our people are like this, basically gay and colourful, but with an underlying note of sadness in their lives. There is so much here that needs improving upon.'

'Ah, you're a radical!' exclaimed Toni, laughing. 'I had thought it would be impossible to find that kind of attitude amongst the – how shall I put it – aristocracy of this country.'

'Oh, but why?' exclaimed Isabel. 'We are not blind to the misery we can find in our streets. But such reforms are enormously difficult to achieve.'

'Yes,' Toni nodded. 'Nevertheless, here there are such tremendous extremes – the very rich, and the very poor.'

'And who can say who is the happier?' remarked the Conde, joining them, standing lazily beside Toni's seat, a drink between his long fingers. 'You are of that breed of people who cannot see that all things are relative.'

Toni flushed. 'That's the kind of defence always put up by – by – such as you,' she replied, bending her head.

'J – Janet!' exclaimed Paul.

'Be still, Paul!' The Conde's eyes were narrowed. 'Your – fiancée interests me greatly. Do go on. Explain yourself, *senhorita*.'

Toni lifted her shoulders, aware now that she had the attention of the whole party. She saw Francesca watching her, her expression amused and insolent and her defiance hardened.

'What more is there to say?' she asked coolly, challenging the Conde with the clear green transparency of her eyes. 'Surely I've said it all. What I would like to know is how you can say so carelessly that all things are relative. What proof have you of this?'

The Conde moved indolently, and Toni was reminded of the lithe, supple menace of a jungle beast. '*Senhorita*,' he said softly, 'I do not have to prove myself to you. Can you deny, however, that during the course of one's life, one's needs, one's pleasures, change? You, for instance, would not enjoy – candybars, trips to the zoo, a new teddy bear, today. Your – shall we say – pleasures are more sophisticated. You enjoy a – cigarette, a touch from a lover's lips, a caress. . . .' His voice was deliberately soft and taunting, and Toni shivered. 'But can you also say, in all sincerity, that these more sophisticated pleasures give you more – physical and mental enjoyment than the simpler, childish things you used to do?'

Toni shook her head. 'Go on.'

The Conde smiled. 'So then is life relative. A millionaire gets pleasure from his money, from his yachts, his private plane, perhaps. The poor man enjoys simpler things, but with no less satisfaction.'

'Poverty can't be dismissed so easily,' retorted Toni, ignoring Paul's scandalized gesticulations.

'I do not dismiss it, *senhorita*.' The Conde's voice was cold now. 'There is no poverty on my estates. Nevertheless, in all walks of life there must be the servant and the master. Without both of these nothing would be accomplished. The gulf between the two is greater in some places than in others, but the principle works equally well.'

'A kind of dictatorship, in fact.'

'Would you rather have the kind of groping incompetence one finds when a man tries to do a job he cannot do? Or the organized expertise of the specialist?'

'I suppose it's a case of better the devil you know,' remarked Toni dryly, and was pleased when the Conde's eyes darkened ominously.

'*Senhorita*—' he began, when Laura Passamentes came up to him, sliding a possessive arm through his.

'Raoul, *querido*,' she murmured gently. 'I think your position is quite clear.' She glanced contemptuously at Toni. 'If the *senhorita* does not accept it, she is merely one alone in her beliefs. Can we not dance a little?'

The Conde's expression changed, and Toni noticed that his scar which had seemed so pronounced a few moments ago relaxed a little as the Conde himself relaxed. He looked down at Laura with a softened expression, and Toni bent her head, not watching them. There was something intimate about that look and she could not understand her own revulsion at the sight.

Later in the evening, while Paul was dancing with Isabel, Toni found herself studying the Conde's scar, pondering on its origin. Obviously, he could have had plastic surgery to remove the scar completely, but he chose not to do so, and because of it had added something infinitely disturbing to his features. Then she found his eyes upon her, and she quickly looked away.

Leaving the lounge she walked along the corridor which she had found led to the huge banqueting hall of the castle where they had first entered the building. The passage was lit at intervals by electric candles in sconces. The hall itself, when she pushed open the heavy doors, was deserted and she walked in with some pleasure, glad of the opportunity to explore alone. The coat of arms over the fireplace was, she realized, a larger replica of the shield the Conde had on his car, and looked magnificent in crimson and silver. She studied it for a moment before turning to look at the heavy oak table and matching chairs. The rugs on the floor, some of which still were attached to the animals' heads, gave the place a medieval air, and she wondered what nights of beer drinking and debauchery had preceded the present empty grandeur of the hall. She could picture the table, heavily laden with meat and fruit, silver goblets overflowing with red wine, serving wenches and soldiers. . . . Her thoughts were real and imaginative, and she did not hear the doors open and close until someone said:

'What is wrong, *senhorita*? Has our small difference of opinion destroyed your taste for company?'

Toni swung round, her hair framing her lightly tanned features.

'You wouldn't be following me, *senhor*?' she countered, with an attempt at a coolness she did not feel.

He did not answer, but merely moved further into the hall, looking tall, and lean and attractive. Toni put a hand to her throat, and turned away, deliberately pretending to examine the wall tapestry nearby which depicted a typical hunting scene. He joined her, standing beside her, watching the fleeting expressions which crossed her face so revealingly.

'You like my castle, *senhorita*?' he asked softly.

'Of course. Anyone would.' Toni was abrupt.

'Not anyone, not everyone. Paul has little time for the – how shall I put it? – beautiful things in life. To him things must be taken, or used, or destroyed. Never simply appreciated.'

Toni looked up at him curiously. 'You haven't much of an opinion of Paul, have you?' She frowned. 'Why?'

The Conde shrugged his shoulders. 'It is not for me to destroy *your* illusions, *senhorita*.'

Toni compressed her lips for a moment. 'You wouldn't, anyway,' she said sharply. 'What has he done? Heavens, he's barely thirty, too young to have lived a life so objectionable to yourself!'

The Conde's eyes narrowed. '*Senhorita*, you obviously have no conception of what you are talking about, and I suggest you keep your opinions to yourself. My reasons for not – liking – my nephew are all mine, and I do not wish to discuss them.'

Toni gave an exasperated sigh. 'Your – your sister must be quite a lot older than you are,' she probed.

'Paul's mother is exactly ten years older than myself,' he returned smoothly, 'though why that should interest you I cannot imagine.'

Toni thought about that. It made the Conde about thirty-nine or forty. Physically, he looked younger, but mentally she thought he was fully aware of the vagaries of life which only experience can teach you. She wondered whether his antipathy towards Paul had anything to do with Paul's mother, his sister. Maybe he was like his father, ingrained with family concerns, unwilling to admit a stranger to their midst. And yet he had married a Frenchwoman, so Paul had said, and that didn't quite add up. She thought of Francesca's fanatical devotion to her father, and for the first time felt the faint glimmerings of understanding towards the girl. Her father was not the kind of man to live the life of a celibate, and maybe she was afraid he might marry someone entirely unsuitable. Toni sighed. It was not her problem, yet she was making it so.

Now she began to walk slowly towards the door. 'Are you leaving, *senhorita*?' he asked mockingly. 'Does my presence annoy you? Or disturb you?'

Toni swung round. 'You don't disturb me, *senhor*,' she exclaimed vehemently.

'No?'

'No. Only in so far as I cannot understand your bigoted attitude.'

The Conde's eyes were dark with anger, and she felt a curious feeling, a mixture of fear and excitement, at the knowledge that she knew very little of this man whose emotions could erupt with such violence.

He took a step towards her, but suddenly she was really afraid, and without waiting for his reply, she fled out of the door, and along the corridor towards the lounge. In her haste, she did not see the girl approaching from the opposite direction and almost ran into Francesca. Francesca stared at her in astonishment, but Toni had no time to care about the possible effects of her actions on Francesca. She had the strangest feeling of claustrophobia and she had to escape from the suffocated breathlessness she was enduring.

'*Senhorita*, is something wrong?' Francesca's lips tightened.

Toni stared at her, shaking her head, and biting her lips. 'No – no – of course, nothing is wrong!' she murmured. 'Excuse me!'

Francesca watched her until she was out of sight, a cold mask enfolding her young face.

CHAPTER FIVE

THE next day Paul told her that the Conde had left for Lisbon again. Toni felt a sense of relief, and yet the Conde's presence had given her a kind of stimulation it was difficult to understand.

'When are we leaving, Paul?' she asked bluntly. 'We've been here four days already. You told me it was only to be a short visit.'

Paul moved restlessly. They were sitting on the beach below the *castelo*, the sun warm on their bare shoulders. He opened his cigarette case and extracted two, handing one to Toni thoughtfully.

'What's the hurry?' he parried. 'You said yourself you've no job to go back to. I would have thought you would appreciate not having anything to do but eat, sleep and lie in the sun.'

Toni leaned forward to light her cigarette, then blew the smoke into the air reflectively. 'You shouldn't speculate about me, Paul. I'm not like you. That was always the trouble. You always thought you knew best, for both of us.'

'But you do like it here?'

Toni shrugged. 'I like the *castelo* and naturally I like the climate. As to the rest – well, the Condessa is kind and friendly, but I see little of her. Francesca is openly antagonistic!'

'And Raoul?' Paul's eyes were intent. 'He's your real

problem, isn't he?'

Toni shaded her eyes and looked out to sea. 'Not particularly.'

Paul looked disgruntled. 'Oh, don't give me that, Toni, *please*! I'm not blind, you know!'

'Just what do you mean by that?'

Paul's lips twisted. 'You know perfectly well what I mean, Toni Morley! Your conversation with my dear uncle last night did not go unnoticed!' He snorted. 'Not only by me, I might add. Laura didn't like it either. No one, but no one, argues with the Conde della Maria Estrada!'

Toni bent her head, running a hand under the weight of her hair. 'Is that so? And what did you all gather from it, then?'

Paul grimaced. 'Obviously, you're attracted by him.'

'What!' Toni stared at him.

'Sure. Even I don't need to be drawn a picture, Toni. I may be thick in some ways, but in this, so far as you're concerned, I'm perceptive.'

'Then you're allowing your perception to lead you astray,' retorted Toni hotly. 'Your uncle is of no interest to me, except in as much as he intrigues me by his obvious antagonism towards you. Why? What has he got against you? Apart from your obvious desire to increase your financial status at the expense of your grandmother?'

Paul lay back, blowing smoke-rings into the air. 'Why should there be anything else?'

'Because he's not a stupid man! Whatever else he may be, he has concrete reasons for not wanting you here, and I'd like to know what they are.'

'I guess you would at that!' Paul laughed. 'Maybe you have some ideas of your own, Toni. After all, Uncle Raoul has everything going for him, hasn't he? Attraction, if you can ignore that distortion of his face by the famous scar! A beautiful home, that appeals to you artistically! And finally, an income in the region of a hundred thousand a year!'

Toni gave him a scornful glance. 'Oh, Paul, I'd hate to have your mind!' She studied the tip of her cigarette. 'Do you honestly imagine I'd be foolish enough to be interested in a man because of his money?'

'Why not? Thousands of women are!'

'I am not thousands of women. I'm me! I couldn't be like some of these girls who marry men years and years older than themselves in the hope that they'll take a powder in a couple of years, leaving them the usual wealthy widow! I'd hate to have some old man pawing me!' she shivered.

Paul sat up. 'You can hardly put Raoul into that class, darling. And I'm pretty sure you'd like him to – paw you – as you put it!'

Toni's fingers stung across his cheek, and he stared at her furiously as they became aware of a third person crossing the sands towards them.

'You bitch!' muttered Paul, and then Francesca was standing over them, looking down, her expression insolent.

'What's wrong?' she asked sneeringly. 'Dissension in the happy home already?'

'Get lost, Francesca,' muttered Paul, rubbing his

cheek.

'No, don't.' Toni rose to her feet, tall and slim in a dark blue bathing suit. 'Are you going swimming, Francesca?'

Francesca considered her insolently. 'I may be. Why?'

'Can I come with you?'

The girl lifted her shoulders indolently, and then a narrowed expression in her eyes brought a reluctant reply. 'I suppose so. I'm going to the rock basin.'

Paul stood up too. '*Janet!*' he said harshly.

Toni wrinkled her nose at him, and turning walked away with Francesca without looking back. They crossed the mossy, slippery rocks at the far side of the beach and came upon a natural basin some twenty feet across which provided a perfect swimming pool. Toni dropped the towel she was carrying, and without waiting for Francesca, she dived into the cool depths. The water was sun-warm and creamed over her hot limbs like satin. She surfaced, shaking back her long hair which she had secured with the usual elastic bands. Francesca was still standing on the rocks, watching her. She had shed her own wrap to reveal a rather demure suit in black and white stripes, with broad shoulder straps that looked old-fashioned and clumsy.

'Are you coming in?' asked Toni breathlessly, gulping the fresh air into her lungs.

Francesca shrugged. 'You swim well,' she said grudgingly, and Toni wondered why there should be a note of such disappointment in her voice. 'Be careful, *senhorita*. The pool is very deep!'

Toni sighed. 'I'm not afraid, Francesca. Sorry to disappoint you.'

Francesca lifted her shoulders. 'Why did you come with me, *senhorita*? What were you and Paul arguing about?'

'That's our affair,' Toni replied shortly. Really, these della Maria Estradas were impossible! Did they think they had the right of kings to ask such personal questions?

'I think it was to do with my father,' said Francesca angrily, her cheeks flushed. 'Something happened last night, didn't it?'

'Oh, really, Francesca, stop trying to understand adult complexities. You're no psychiatrist, and nothing happened last evening. Nothing at all!'

Francesca sat down, dangling her legs in the water. 'You're lying,' she said sullenly. 'You are not fooling me for one moment. You're becoming involved with my father, aren't you?'

'Oh, lord!' Toni raised her eyes heavenward. 'Does everybody's mind revolve around the same dreary topic?'

Francesca's eyes flashed. 'So! That is what you and Paul were arguing about!'

'I didn't say that.'

'No, but you said enough, *senhorita*. What is the matter? Is one man not good enough for you?'

'Francesca, one day you'll drive me too far,' muttered Toni furiously. 'You're thirteen. For goodness' sake stop behaving like a spoilt baby!'

'But you must admit you do deliberately annoy my

father,' exclaimed Francesca. 'He left this morning for Lisbon. He was not expected to leave for several days. Now why should he do that?'

'Heavens, I don't know. I'm not his keeper.'

'It's like I said, something happened between you two last night.'

'Oh, don't be *stupid*!'

Toni swam across to her impatiently. 'Francesca, please, can't we be friends? There isn't such a great gap in our ages, we could have such fun together.'

She looked up at the girl appealingly. Francesca was alone somehow. When her father was around she was happy, but when he left, when he interested himself in something or someone apart from her, she felt lost.

Francesca pouted her mouth. 'Go away, *senhorita*,' she muttered sulkily. 'I do not wish to be your friend. *I hate you!*'

Toni stared at her. 'Don't be so silly, Francesca.'

'I'm not silly. It is you who are silly, *senhorita*. Imagining that my father would interest himself in a nonentity like *you*!'

Toni grasped Francesca's ankle angrily, intending to pull her down into the water and thus halt this horrible conversation. But Francesca was stronger than she thought, and remained firm, kicking out with her leg and throwing Toni back with violent force. Toni gave a gasp of surprise, and then there was an awful blinding pain and the pounding of water in her ears, before she knew no more.

She was lying on something soft, and her body felt

weak and helpless, but her head hurt, terribly, as though she was resting it on a bed of nails, and one nail in particular was digging into her with persistent pressure. When she tried to move the pain grew unbearable, and she uttered a faint cry that sounded like thunder in her ears.

She felt something cool on her forehead, and a voice very faintly soothing. Everything was blue and her eyelids seemed stuck so that she could not open them. The effort to do so was too much for her, and she felt blackness overwhelming the blueness.

Then later she found she could open her eyes, and as things swam into focus, she distinguished the uniformed figure of a nurse seated beside her bed, who noticed her awakening at once, and came over to look down at her with anxious eyes.

'*Senhorita!*' she said. 'How do you feel?'

Toni swallowed with difficulty. 'A drink,' she murmured hoarsely, 'could I have a drink?'

'Of course. A moment, *senhorita.*'

The water was sweet and reviving, and Toni relaxed back on her pillow tiredly. 'Wh ... where am I?' she murmured.

'At the Castelo Estrada, *senhorita*. Surely you remember. You were swimming. . . .'

Toni tried to think but the effort hurt her, and she shook her head slowly. 'Tell me, please,' she whispered. 'What happened?'

The nurse smoothed her forehead with a cooling towel. 'Later, *senhorita*, later,' she said, smiling a little. 'Relax, and I will ask the doctor to come and see you.'

Toni felt her eyelids closing after the nurse had gone, and she tried to keep them open, but after a moment she was asleep. When she opened her eyes again she found the room dark, only a lamp by her bed illuminating the scene. The nurse was still there, but her face had changed, and she realized it was another nurse entirely. The room, too, became familiar to her. It was her room. She was at the *castelo*, with Paul – Paul Craig. Yes, that was right. Paul Craig.

The nurse came over to her. 'So you're awake again, Senhorita West,' she said.

West? West? Toni's mind rejected the name. Her name was not West. It was Morris – no, Morley; yes, that was right, Morley. She opened her mouth to deny her identity, when she remembered the deception Paul had induced her to share. They thought she was called West, Janet West. Thank goodness she had remembered in time!

The nurse put a cup to her lips and she sipped gratefully, then asked: 'How long have I been here?'

'Not long,' said the nurse reassuringly. 'Do you remember what happened?'

Toni tried to think again, but now it was all clearer. 'Y-e-s,' she said slowly, 'I – I think so. I – I was swimming. Francesca was there.'

'That's right. You fell, and hit your head on the rocks. Francesca saved your life. You would have drowned!'

'I – I would?' Toni frowned, trying to bring every detail into perspective. 'Yes – I would. I remember now. . . .'

She remembered what had happened. She had not

96

slipped and fallen. Francesca had pushed her away, with her foot. She must have hit her head on a rock. She could remember the pounding in her ears and she shivered.

'You're cold?' asked the nurse quickly. 'No?'

'No,' replied Toni, shaking her head. 'No.' She sighed, and managed a faint smile.

The nurse gave a reassuring pat to her shoulder. 'Wait a moment, *senhorita*. Try not to sleep while I fetch Doctor Rodrigues.'

Now it was much easier to stay awake, and Toni moved her head very slowly on the pillow to look towards the door. What a shock Francesca must have had. How frightened she must have felt!

A white uniform heralded the return of the nurse accompanied by a small, dapper little man with a moustache. He came briskly over to the bed, giving Toni the ghost of a smile as he asked the nurse a lot of questions in their own language. Toni tried to follow them, but it was impossible for her to do so. Then Doctor Rodrigues placed a thermometer under her tongue and took her pulse with expert precision.

'Good, good!' he said at last. 'I am glad you are feeling a little better, Senhorita West. You gave us quite a shock, but I am happy to say you are improving with satisfactory speed.'

Toni ran her tongue over her dry lips. 'Thank you.'

The nurse smiled down at her. 'Would you like something to eat? Some soup perhaps?'

Toni nodded. 'Please. I do feel rather empty. How long have I been lying here?'

The doctor frowned. 'Just a little over twenty-four hours, *senhorita*,' he replied. 'It is usual when one has concussion as you had that the consciousness rejects the discomfort. You have two stitches in the back of your head, *senhorita*. That is why your head is so sore.'

'Oh!' Toni couldn't quite assimilate this. She had actually been unconscious for the better part of a whole day and night! It seemed incredible.

'So now Nurse Gonzales will bring you some soup, and I will see you again tomorrow,' said the doctor. '*Boa noite, senhorita.*'

After the doctor and the nurse had both gone, the nurse to get the soup, Toni tried to struggle up a little on her pillows. A wave of giddiness overwhelmed her and she broke out in a cold sweat with the nauseating dizziness. She sank back weakly, as the door opened to admit the Conde della Maria Estrada.

She stared at him in astonishment. 'But – but you're in Lisbon!' she said disbelievingly, almost believing she was having delusions.

'*Was* in Lisbon,' returned the Conde smoothly, closing the door and leaning back against it.

Toni's fingers clenched under the bedcovers. 'What do you want, *senhor*?'

'Is it not conceivable that I might be concerned as to your welfare?' he said harshly.

'Frankly, no,' said Toni, closing her eyes for a moment, and then opening them swiftly as she heard movements and found him beside the bed. 'N-Nurse Gonzales will be back in a moment with some soup,' she continued, refusing to meet his eyes.

'I know it. How do you feel?' His eyes were intent.

Toni moved her head from side to side. 'All right, I guess.' She was trembling. 'I wish you would go away. You make me nervous.'

'Why? Why should I do that, *senhorita*?' The Conde thrust his hands deep into the pockets of his trousers. 'Unless, perhaps, you have something to hide?'

Toni's eyes flew open, staring at him in dismay. 'I – I have nothing to hide, *senhor*.'

'Haven't you?' He looked sceptical. 'You are not a convincing liar, Senhorita *Morley*.'

Toni felt the pain in her head intensify. She winced, and closed her eyes, and as she did so the door re-opened to admit the nurse.

'Oh!' The nurse was embarrassed. '*Desculpe*, Senhor Conde. I did not realize—'

'*Esta bem*, Senhorita Gonzales,' murmured the Conde, his tone light and smooth, much different from the cold insensitivity of his words to Toni. 'I am going.' He looked down at Toni as she opened her eyes. 'I will see you later, *senhorita*!'

Toni did not reply and after he had gone, closing the door behind him, Nurse Gonzales studied her patient with more concern. 'The – er – the Senhor Conde was concerned about you?' There was a questioning tone to her voice.

Toni sighed. 'Maybe,' she said wearily, and the nurse did not press her further.

The effort of drinking the soup exhausted her, and despite the disturbing turmoil of her thoughts she slept again. Now she was floating in a green world; there was

99

water everywhere, pouring into her ears, her eyes, her throat, choking her! She awoke, sweating, her heart pounding in her ears.

Now it was light; the shutters were thrust open and a faint breeze off the sea fanned her forehead. She relaxed, and as she calmed down she realized that the pain in her head had eased considerably. Now there was only a dull ache, and she moved quite easily, stretching her legs, and bringing her arms out of the covers.

The room was empty, but presently the door was pushed open slowly, and a face appeared. It was Francesca, and Toni looked at her, noticing the faint lines of strain around her eyes. She looked pale, and Toni wondered what had caused her such concern. Surely not her own condition; she doubted that even Francesca's part in the whole affair would give her so much anxiety.

'Come in, Francesca,' said Toni, struggling up on her pillows with difficulty.

Francesca hesitated a moment, then advanced into the room. She walked indolently, a sullen expression as usual marring the smooth features. She did not speak, and Toni swallowed hard and said:

'I'm sorry if I caused you a deal of trouble, Francesca.'

The girl shrugged her shoulders. 'You didn't trouble me,' she denied coolly.

'Well, at least, I have you to thank for saving my life,' said Toni patiently.

Francesca gave a short laugh. 'Yes, I did that,' she said coldly. 'I had no desire to have you on my conscience!'

Toni gave an exasperated gasp. 'Honestly, Francesca, you really are the limit! Why have you come here? Just to try and intimidate me?'

The girl fingered the bedcovers without giving any thought to the action. She seemed thoughtful and withdrawn, and Toni thought she had probably come to make sure she was really recovering. After all, in spite of her denials of caring whether or not Toni was alive or dead, she was still very young, and not everything she said was really meant.

If only there was some way to reach her, thought Toni regretfully. No young thing was ever all bad and Francesca had proved she had all the normal reactions to circumstances.

'Why did my father come to see you?' she asked suddenly, and Toni was taken aback.

'Well, I guess he came to see how I was,' said Toni awkwardly, not wanting to think about the Conde, and the possible outcome of his knowledge of her identity.

Francesca chewed her lip. 'Why should he care?'

'Oh, lord!' Toni shook her head. 'I don't imagine he gives a damn,' she exclaimed. 'However, I was a guest in his home at the time of the accident, and I suppose, like you, he didn't want me on his conscience!'

Francesca considered this. 'But why did he come back from Lisbon? He could have telephoned,' she persisted. 'After all, Doctor Rodrigues was called immediately, and he himself informed my father of the – accident.'

Toni couldn't answer this. She could hardly explain

to Francesca that her father had returned to confront an impostor in his home, without revealing the full circumstances of the affair, which she was not at liberty to do. It was up to Paul to explain. Indeed, she would be glad if it all were resolved. There were too many undercurrents here, and she wanted to get away before they overpowered her completely. She didn't know why she felt so strongly about it. She had never considered herself an hysterical, imaginative person, and yet the Conde della Maria Estrada aroused the most peculiar sensations inside her.

Francesca moved restlessly about the room, picking up perfume sprays and hand-creams, studying them intently for a moment, and then putting them down again.

'Estevan thinks you're marvellous,' she said, rather mockingly.

Toni did not reply, and the girl gave her a baleful look.

'When are you and Paul leaving here?'

Toni gave a helpless shrug. 'I – I wish I could tell you,' she murmured regretfully.

'Why? Don't pretend you want to leave!'

'Oh, but I do,' exclaimed Toni. 'However, I can't say for certain, not now – with this.' She indicated her head. 'But I promise we'll be leaving just as soon as we can.'

'Good.' Francesca folded her arms and studied the girl in the bed. 'I shall be glad when the *castelo* is quiet again.'

Toni ran her tongue over her dry lips. 'Then maybe

you will get a governess,' she suggested casually.

Francesca scowled. 'I do not need a governess, *senhorita.*'

'That is not what our grandmother says, *querida,*' remarked Paul's mocking voice behind her.

Francesca swung round. 'You know nothing about it,' she said angrily. 'Why do you persist in staying here, interfering in our affairs? You know my father does not like you!'

'No, I agree, your father does not,' returned Paul. 'However, your father is not the kind of man to prevent a grandson from visiting his grandmother. Whatever his personal reasons for wanting me to stay away may be.'

'And what are those personal reasons?' asked Toni tiredly.

'Wouldn't you like to know!' said Francesca mockingly. 'Hasn't Paul told you about them?'

'Francesca!' muttered Paul warningly. Toni watched this interplay curiously.

'Oh, don't worry, I shan't tell her,' said Francesca contemptuously. 'Let her find out for herself what kind of man she is marrying!'

'*Francesca!*' Paul was white with anger, and Toni wondered what on earth all this was about. However, Francesca apparently decided she had done enough, for she turned and flounced out of the room, leaving them alone. Immediately, Paul relaxed, but Toni stretched out a warning hand towards him, saying:

'Your uncle knows my name is not Janet West!'

Paul gave an involuntary gasp. 'What!'

'You heard me,' said Toni wearily. 'Your uncle knows my real name.'

'But how?' Paul shook his head in amazement. 'Did you—?'

'Of course not!' Toni looked annoyed. 'Why should I want to tell *him* the truth?'

Paul hunched his shoulders. 'I don't intend having another argument about that!' he muttered, and Toni widened her eyes indignantly.

'Well, anyway,' she said, 'as he knows who I am, we'd better get away from here as soon as I'm capable of making the journey!'

Paul grunted moodily. 'I bet he's been snooping around trying to find out all about you – even as Janet West, he wouldn't be content until he discovered something he could tell my grandmother.'

Toni looked impatient. 'Do you really imagine your uncle has nothing better to do than worry about some stupid girl you brought here?'

'No, but – oh, anyway, he has his reasons for not wanting me here!'

'So it would appear.' Toni moved restlessly. 'Oh, go away, Paul, you infuriate me at times. I wish I'd never agreed to this crazy masquerade!'

Paul walked to the door, and then looked back at her. 'Just remember, Toni, when you're making these assessments of my character, that you agreed to come here. I didn't tie you up and kidnap you!'

'I know it. Unfortunately.' Toni turned on to her side, wincing as the stitches pained her. 'Go away, Paul, just go away!'

Paul left as Nurse Gonzales came back. She fussed over Toni, smiling at her benevolently, obviously under the mistaken impression that Toni was a person of some importance. How wrong can you be? thought Toni cynically, as a procession of tortuous thoughts paraded through her tired mind. What would Paul tell his grandmother? And would the Conde think it necessary to punish them in some way for trying to cheat him? It was an awful situation, and she was glad when her tiredness overwhelmed her and she slept again.

Two days later Toni was up and about her room. Her strength was returning rapidly. After all, she was a young healthy animal, and although she had lost quite a lot of blood, the bed-rest had almost cured her. In addition the sea air worked wonders, and she sat by her window, gazing out at the sun-kissed scene of beach and shoreline and sky, and could almost feel content.

During the two days, the Condessa had been a regular visitor, spending some time with her during the late afternoon and early evening. She obviously as yet knew nothing of her son's revelations, and she treated Toni so kindly that the girl felt painfully ashamed of the deception she was practising.

Paul did not return, nor did Francesca. She was not surprised that Francesca stayed away – after all, the girl had made it plain that she disliked Toni intensely, and did not trust her either. But Paul was different, and Toni pondered his absence with some misgivings. Possibly Paul was taking every opportunity of depriving his grandmother of some of her wealth, and time spent with his co-called fiancée was merely wasted.

Yet Toni felt afraid that Paul might be attempting to ignore what she had told him, and carry on with the deception in the face of his uncle's contempt. Maybe he thought his uncle would not tell his grandmother in case such news upset her; maybe he was banking on that. Toni was nauseated by the whole affair. She just wanted to get away, and every time her door opened she expected the Conde to appear and wreak some frightful wrath upon her.

Four days after her accident, when she was sitting by her window in the late afternoon dressed only in a dark blue quilted housecoat, her silvery hair loose about her shoulders, the Conde arrived.

Toni knew who it was almost before the door opened. She heard the firm footsteps, and felt the familiar feeling of nervousness that descended upon her now at his appearance. This time he knocked at her door before entering, but she had barely time to bid him enter before he did so.

She glanced round. Today, dressed in a biscuit-coloured lounge suit, his thick hair combed smoothly, he looked every inch the Portuguese aristocrat that he was, and Toni trembled a little as he came to stand in front of her.

'Well, *senhorita*,' he said, surveying her with those intensely dark eyes, 'you look much better.'

Toni swallowed. 'Oh – yes, *senhor*, I am – much better!'

'Good – good, I am glad.'

Toni looked up at him squarely. 'Are you?'

He smiled faintly and mockingly. 'Oh, yes, *senhorita*. Be assured of it.'

Toni bent her head, unwillingly aware that his nearness caused the strangest sensations inside her. Whether her illness had weakened her or not she was not sure, yet she felt hot all over, and could not meet his penetrating gaze.

He moved to the window, and leaned back against it, arms folded, studying her. She looked up uncomfortably, and then said with some defiance:

'Don't look at me like that!'

'You don't like me to look at you, *senhorita*?'

'No. Not like that!'

'Like what?'

Toni's cheeks burned. 'You know what I mean, *senhor*. Please, say what you have to say, and go.'

'But I am enjoying looking at you, *senhorita*. After all, your discomfort is merely a confirmation to me of your own guilt. Poor Senhorita Morley, you did not think to be found out – and so soon in our relationship!'

Toni clenched her fists. 'You are insolent, *senhor*!' She shivered. 'You wouldn't speak to me like this if your mother were here – if Paul were here!'

'No,' he inclined his head in agreement. 'But they are not here, and I am free to say what I like to a woman – such as you!'

Toni got shakily to her feet. 'What do you mean? A woman such as me?'

'My opinion of your sex has not been a favourable one for many years now, *senhorita*, and your charade with my nephew has not endeared them to me. No, *senhorita*, there are few women who are worthy of a man's trust.' His scar stood out starkly, and Toni wondered again how it had appeared there.

She swayed now. '*Senhor*, your opinion of me is not important!'

'You are wrong, *senhorita*. It is very important – in some ways. The morals of a woman are always important!'

'My God!' Toni shook her head. 'What am I supposed to have done? Pretended to be Paul's fiancée, that's all. Is that a crime? I haven't seduced him or anything.'

He caught her angrily by the shoulders, shaking her violently. 'I will tell you, *senhorita*, what you have done. You attempted to seduce the husband of a good friend of mine – Miguel de Calle!'

He let her go, and she fell, supporting herself weakly against the chair. 'You – you're crazy,' she gasped. 'I didn't do that!' She moved her head helplessly. 'Your friend believes what it suits her to believe! That is the truth!'

The Conde looked derisive. 'You are telling me that Miguel forced his attentions on you? That he ignored Estelle, his wife, to attempt to make love to his children's governess?'

'Yes. That's exactly what he did do!' Toni was pale.

The Conde gave a shake of his head. 'Oh, *senhorita*, do you think I am fool? Do I look so gullible? Am I perhaps still wet behind the ears? No! No, *senhorita*, I am not a fool. Miguel is a rich man. A woman like you would not object to a rich man's attentions, should he find you attractive!'

Toni was aghast. 'How dare you!'

'You will find, *senhorita*, that I dare a lot of things!' He linked his hard fingers about her slim wrist, drawing her relentlessly towards him. Toni struggled desperately, trying to free herself, but she was close against the muscular length of his body and the movements did peculiar things to her metabolism. Her breath was swift and breathing was difficult; she could feel the smooth, expensive material of his suit, and smell the faint odour of shaving lotion and the heat of his body; his hand hurt her as it twisted her arm a little cruelly behind her, but his mouth disturbed her most of all. It was only inches above her own, smiling mockingly, his eyes darkened with contempt. 'So, *senhorita*,' he murmured, 'what do you say now?'

Toni felt her head throbbing, but as swiftly was aware of the change in his attitude. One moment he was holding her mockingly, derisively, jeering at her futile attempts to free herself, and the next his eyes had strange lights dancing in their depths, and his hold brought her closer against the firm hardness of his body. He stared at her for a heart-stopping moment, shaking his head slowly, and then with a muffled exclamation he bent his head and she felt the searing pressure of his mouth parting her own.

It was the kind of lovemaking Toni had never experienced. She had thought she knew almost everything about kissing, but she at once realized how mistaken she had been. There was an expertise in his touch that aroused her to the full awareness of her own body and its needs, and she felt her resistance slipping away from her. Instead of struggling, she wanted to wind her arms about his neck and let him have his way with her. Gone was the arrogant, self-controlled Conde della Maria Estrada, and in his place was a man, with a man's desires and appetites that hungered for satisfaction. When Toni had almost forgotten everything, her surroundings, her antagonism towards this man, and most important of all his contempt for her, he thrust her savagely away from him, a cruel smile twisting his mouth.

Toni swayed on her feet, grasping the chair to support herself, while he continued to stare at her with mocking eyes. 'So, *senhorita*,' he said, harshly, 'it is as I thought. You do not find my lovemaking so unpleasant!'

Toni buried her face in her hands. 'Go away,' she muttered unsteadily. 'Go away!'

The Conde straightened, and smoothed his hair with a lazy hand. 'I will go when I am ready, *senhorita*. And now you cannot deny that I have proved my point.'

Toni looked up wearily. 'What point?'

'That you are weak and promiscuous!' He drew out his cigarette case, extracted one, and lit it with deliberate ease. Then he looked at her through a haze of blue smoke. 'Nevertheless, I cannot deny that you are a – how shall I put it? – beautiful woman,' he spoke dispassionately, surveying her appraisingly, 'and maybe

Miguel would not require too much encouragement—'

'I did not encourage him!' Toni clenched her fists. 'For heaven's sake, *senhor*, leave me alone! I didn't want to come here in the first place, and I will leave as soon as I'm able!' She stiffened her back. 'And don't think because I'm incumbent upon your generosity that you are entitled to treat me as you will! Whatever your misconceived beliefs may be, I do not subscribe to them!'

He gave an amused laugh. '*Senhorita*, you are unique! You expect me to believe your story when I have it from Miguel de Calle himself that you deliberately tried to entice him into your bedroom—'

'*What!*' Toni was horrified.

'*Sim!* Do not bother to deny it again. Did I not myself witness the predicament you had got yourself into that day in Lisbon? Another case of mistaken encouragement, no doubt! What a record you have, *senhorita*! Not content with this, you then come here posing as my nephew's fiancée. Unfortunately, for you, Senhora Passamentes is a close friend of Estelle de Calle. She remembered vaguely seeing you there, and after I had checked her story with the de Calles, your masquerade was over.'

Toni sank down on to the chair. That was why Laura Passamentes had seemed familiar that night! Naturally, as the children's governess she had had no direct contact with guests in the house, but she would be seen about her duties.

She looked up. 'All right, all right,' she said, shaking her head. 'I don't want to hear any more. I've said I'll leave as soon as I can. But as Paul hasn't been to see me for days we haven't been able to finalize the arrangements.'

The Conde walked lazily towards the door. 'Paul has returned – to England, I imagine,' he remarked coolly. 'He left three days ago. *You* are staying!'

'What!' Toni stood up again. 'What do you mean? I won't stay here, whatever nefarious plans are running through your mind!' Her head was throbbing quite badly now, and she couldn't assimilate this sudden change of events.

'Oh, but you will, *senhorita*. I will explain the details at some later date, when you are more able to understand—'

Toni felt sick. 'But I don't want to stay here,' she exclaimed, panicking a little without really knowing why.

'Maybe not, at the moment,' he murmured softly. 'but you will.'

'But – but – if Paul has left, how can I stay here? What – what will Francesca say? Or your mother?'

The Conde smiled sardonically. 'Oh, didn't I tell you?' he said lazily. 'You're to be Francesca's new governess!'

CHAPTER SIX

WITHIN a week Toni felt completely normal again, if achieving a recovery from the severe knock on her head was feeling completely normal. She felt stronger and could leave her room without feeling tired, except in the evenings, and she had already been down to the beach alone, and paddled in the clear warm water. They were like days out of time, she thought to herself. She was left almost entirely to herself, except for meals, which she shared with either Francesca, the Condessa, or both. The Conde had returned to Lisbon, she was informed, and as the Condessa continued to call her Janet she assumed the rest of the family had not been informed of her altered status. It was all strange and incredible, and she sometimes wondered if she had dreamt that scene in her room when the Conde had held her in his arms and made savage, passionate love to her, before lashing her with his tongue and then astounding her by telling her she was to be Francesca's governess. It was all too fantastic, but as yet she had not the strength to make any definite arrangements about leaving, so she stayed on, and continued to play her part.

Of course, that didn't stop her from wondering why Paul had left so abruptly. Surely he hadn't given up his ideas of becoming rich so easily? It didn't sound at all like Paul, who was nothing if not persistent.

Sighing, she refused to consider the problem any longer, and collecting her swimsuit she made her way down to the beach. Stretched out on the sands she felt warm and content, and could almost forget the disturbing ache she felt in her stomach whenever she thought of the Conde.

Francesca found her there, and sat down beside her, speaking to her for the first time since that day in her bedroom.

'My father rang this morning,' she said thoughtfully, examining a shell with concentrated attention.

'Oh, yes!' Toni was wary. She had not yet recovered from the way these della Maria Estradas treated her.

'Yes. He asked if you were still here.'

Toni felt sarcastic. 'Did he imagine I might leave?'

'No.' Francesca was calm. 'He told me you were staying indefinitely.'

Toni sat up, and rubbed her head a little ruefully as the sudden movement brought a faint pounding. She looked at the girl. 'Did he tell you why?' she asked.

Francesca shrugged. 'He said you were to become my governess. He said your name wasn't Janet West at all, but Antonia Morley. Is that right?'

Toni swallowed. '*Toni* Morley,' she amended slowly. 'No one calls me Antonia.'

Francesca sighed. 'You're not Paul's fiancée, then?'

'No.'

'Does my father—' she flushed, and rested her chin on her updrawn knees, '—does my father – is he – well, are you his mistress?'

Toni's eyes widened. 'No!' Then she frowned. 'But

you said that so calmly. I – I always thought you were – well, jealous of him! Wouldn't you care – if it were true?'

Francesca lifted her shoulders. 'My father told me I was not to question you about – well, personal things. I thought naturally – oh, I don't know what I thought.'

Toni studied the girl compassionately. 'I really believe you do care about your father,' she exclaimed. 'I thought you were rude and spoilt and jealous! But it's not that – is it?'

Francesca looked at her fully. 'I want my father to be *happy*!' she said passionately. 'No one who had anything to do with Paul could make me like them!'

Toni sighed. 'But why? Why? Francesca, tell me why?'

Francesca shook her head. 'No. It's not my story to tell. Besides, like you said, you're not interested in my father.'

Toni knelt on her knees, allowing the sun to beat down on her bare shoulders. 'The only thing is, Francesca, I have no intention of staying here. Of becoming your, or anyone else's, governess, in Portugal!'

The girl looked aghast. 'Oh, but you must, you must!'

'Why must I?'

'Because – well, because *he* said so!'

'Well, *he* will have to find someone else,' retorted Toni shortly. 'I don't want to stay here, and he can't make me!'

Francesca studied the shell again. 'I wouldn't say

that, *senhorita*.'

Toni got to her feet. 'For heaven's sake, call me Toni. I'm sick of hearing that word *senhorita*!'

Francesca shrugged. 'All right. Now where are you going?'

Toni shook her head. 'I don't know. I don't know. Why did Paul leave?'

'My father made him go. He paid him money.'

'What!'

Francesca looked up. 'You didn't expect him to go without money, did you?' she asked, with unexpectedly adult candour.

'I see.' Toni gave a short laugh. 'I wonder why he didn't pay me off?'

Francesca shrugged. 'I don't know. There's something strange about it.'

Toni shivered. Even standing there in the heat of the sun she felt cold. She remembered the Conde too well; he could be completely ruthless, and if her own body aroused him to an acute awareness of her, she was infinitely more vulnerable. She had everything to lose, with a man who thought she was easy game.

She gathered her things together, and Francesca looked up at her with eyes which were uncannily like her father's.

'Don't leave,' she said simply.

Toni stared at her, compassion welling up inside her. The child had had a raw deal with her mother dying like that, and having to live her life with a man who was withdrawn and perhaps embittered by the incident in his life that had scarred him so savagely.

She tried to thrust away these thoughts. When had any of the della Maria Estradas shown any compassion for her, except perhaps the old Condessa?

'Your grandmother—' she began.

'Need never know who you are. You can say you used to teach, before you took up office work. She is out of touch with the modern world. She would have no reason to disbelieve you. If my father says it is so, it is so!'

At the mention of the Conde Toni felt her melting compliance harden into distaste. She would not stay, she *could* not stay. There was too much at stake, and something inside her warned her that it was more than her self-respect.

'I – I must go and get changed,' she said, changing the subject, trying to ignore the pain she glimpsed in Francesca's eyes before the perpetual mask resumed its place.

'Of course, *senhorita*,' she said coldly, and resumed her examination of the sea shells.

Toni hesitated a moment, then without another word turned and walked back to the *castelo*.

However, despite Francesca's attitude on the beach, Toni found in the days that followed that the child followed her almost everywhere, even suggesting they should take walks together, exploring the surrounding countryside. There were horses in stables at the *castelo*, but as Toni had only ridden very occasionally at a riding school, she refused to join Francesca at this particular pastime.

So they walked, and talked, and Toni found Francesca quite a stimulating companion. Once her initial antagonism was conquered she chattered away quite naturally, telling Toni about her previous governess, Mademoiselle Dupont, who had been middle-aged and frumpish, and completely incapable of controlling a high-spirited girl like Francesca.

It was strange, she thought, how Paul's departure had changed the child's personality, but Toni began to feel pangs of anxiety as she realized that soon she must make definite arrangements for leaving herself.

When she mentioned this to Francesca, she frowned, and said: 'I really think you ought to stay until my father comes back from Lisbon.'

Toni shook her head. 'Francesca, the nurse has long gone, and even Doctor Rodrigues admits that I am fully recovered. There's nothing to keep me here. I'm a working girl! I've got to get another job!'

Francesca pouted, displaying the face Toni had grown used to seeing in those early days. 'Why can't you stay here? Surely this job is as good as any other, and I am quite sure the salary will be very generous.'

Toni sighed. 'It's no good, Francesca. Look, you know I came here as Paul's fiancée. It was all supposed to be a bit of a laugh. Nothing serious, you understand. Then when we get here I find that Paul is trying to take his grandmother for every penny he can get, and I wanted to leave – at once. Then there was – well, the accident – and other things, and now I've been here over two weeks and it can't go on.' She hunched her shoulders. 'I don't know why your father sent Paul away, but I do know that I'm not going to be used by him in some nefarious plan that I don't know about. I've had enough of intrigue. As it is I cringe every time your grandmother calls me *Janet*. I want to revert to being *me* again, Toni Morley, a plain, ordinary girl without any pretensions to grandeur. It's no good, Francesca. Can't you try to understand?'

Francesca sighed. 'I'm trying to, Toni, honestly I am. It's just – I want you to stay!'

There was a knock at the door and a maid entered, speaking in Portuguese to Francesca. They were sitting in the lounge reading magazines today, for a heavy mist had descended that morning, and now in the late afternoon the day was dull and dismal. Toni thought it reflected her mood, and she barely listened to what the maid was saying. Then she heard the words Senhora *e* Estevan Passamentes, and frowned.

Francesca glanced at her, as the maid nodded and withdrew. 'Laura Passamentes and Estevan have arrived.'

Toni rose to her feet quickly. 'I'll go to my room.'

Francesca put a hand on her arm. 'Of course you won't. You are not a servant, you are my friend. You will stay and have some afternoon tea with us.'

Toni looked down at the close-fitting navy pants and chunky mustard-coloured sweater she was wearing. Her hair was in a ponytail today, and she looked little older than Francesca. 'Honestly, Francesca,' she was saying awkwardly, 'I'm not dressed for visitors,' when the door opened to admit Laura Passamentes, followed closely by her son.

Francesca gave Toni a rueful smile, then rose to greet her guests. Laura was wearing black again, a black suit of heavy crêpe, that moulded her small, delicately proportioned body. Her hair was a snug black cap against her head, and her face was perfectly made-up. Estevan looked young and boyish, and grinned cheerfully at Francesca.

'Francesca, my dear,' Laura was saying, speaking in English for Toni's benefit. 'It is nice to see you. Estevan was so lost at home today – the weather, you understand, and he begged me to come and visit you.' She gave Estevan a fond smile. 'I couldn't refuse him. Are you well?'

Francesca answered her, asking about Laura's health, and generally behaving as a hostess should. Then Laura turned her attention to Toni, taking in the picture she made, assessing every item of her clothing with an experienced eye.

'So, *senhorita*,' she said, 'you are still here!' There was a veiled insolence behind the words, and Toni flushed uncomfortably. She was aware that Laura must know her true identity, and despise her for her deception.

'Yes, *senhora*,' she replied now. 'But I shall be leaving very soon.'

Laura shrugged her slim shoulders. 'It was – unfortunate – that you should have that accident so – *in*opportunely!'

Francesca glanced at Toni. 'It was as much my fault as – as – Toni's,' she said, turning back to Laura. 'If I had not been careless, Toni would not have slipped.'

Toni smiled at the girl. It was the first time Francesca had admitted her own part in that affair.

'I see.' Laura looked sceptical. 'So it is *Toni* now, is it? You were forced to reveal your true identity, *senhorita*?'

Toni managed a small smile. 'At your instigation – yes, *senhorita*,' she said politely.

Laura looked a little taken aback. 'And your grandmother, Francesca, does she know—'

'No!' Francesca was swift to reply. 'I – I don't think we should tell her. My father will tell her when he considers it necessary.'

Laura shrugged. 'If you say so, *querida*.' She seated herself on a low chair. 'And now – perhaps some tea, *sim*?'

'Oh. Yes, of course.' Francesca rang the bell to summon the maid again. 'I'm sorry.'

Laura looked sympathetically at her, as though condoning her mistake, and Toni felt annoyed. She wanted to leave. She had nothing to say to this woman who seemed to consider Raoul della Maria Estrada her property, and his daughter hers to command.

'Er – I'll go to my room, Francesca,' she was beginning, when Laura shook her head.

'Oh, no, *senhorita*, stay and talk to me. Francesca, perhaps you and Estevan could go and play your records. Then Senhorita – Morley and I can have a little chat.'

Francesca looked at Toni who in turn looked imploringly at her. 'I don't think . . .' she was beginning, when Estevan exclaimed:

'Oh, yes, Fran, let us do that! I don't want any tea anyway.'

Francesca was really left without much choice, and she had to shrug her shoulders and after ordering tea from the maid she and Estevan left Laura and Toni alone.

'Now, *senhorita*,' said Laura smoothly, 'come and sit down. I want to talk to you.'

'What about?' Toni was nervous.

'Oh, this and that. Come, sit down.'

'I'd rather stand, if you don't mind,' replied Toni, gripping the edge of the settee with a rather shaky hand. She had the feeling that this was the real reason why Laura Passamentes had come here. It was not on Estevan's behalf, even though he might enjoy Francesca's company, it was because she wanted to speak to herself, Toni. But why? Why?

Laura Passamentes shrugged again. 'As you wish, *senhorita*,' she said, and taking out a handkerchief, blew her nose very daintily. 'Now, my dear Senhorita Morley, perhaps you will tell me the reason why you are still here when Paul left over a week ago.'

Toni wet her lips with her tongue. 'I – I was not well enough to leave with Paul, *senhora*,' she replied.

'I see. But you are well now, are you not?'

'Yes.'

'Then why are you still here?'

Toni lifted her shoulders. 'Francesca did not want me to leave before her father returned from Lisbon.'

'Why?'

Toni's colour deepened. How could she tell this cold,

aristocratic woman that the man she expected to marry had practically threatened her into staying? So she said: 'I expect she thought it would be more polite.'

Laura Passamentes looked annoyed. 'It would have been more polite, *senhorita*, never to have come here at all, masquerading as Paul's fiancée. I should have thought decency would have prevented you from attempting to gain admittance to another Portuguese home after the trouble you caused in Estelle's life!'

'I caused no trouble in Senhora de Calle's life, *senhora*,' said Toni, forcing herself to remain calm with difficulty. 'Senhor de Calle is lying when he says I attempted to – well, attract him! On the contrary, I repulsed him! Unfortunately, I was unable to prove this!'

'*Senhorita!* You are insolent! Do you honestly expect me to believe that a – a – creature like yourself could attract a man of intelligence and breeding like Miguel de Calle?'

Toni bit hard at her lips. 'It is of complete indifference to me what you believe, *senhora*,' she said shortly, trying to prevent the surge of anger that was engulfing her in its grip.

'Is it? Is it indeed? I suggest you go now and pack your suitcases and Estevan and myself will deposit you at the nearest railway station where you may catch a train back to Lisbon!'

Toni's eyes were astounded. 'You can't be serious, *senhora*,' she gasped. 'Why, you have no jurisdiction here! I shall go when I choose – or whenever the Conde considers it necessary!' Her tone was cool and polite.

The girl's self-possession infuriated the hot-tempered Laura, and she rose angrily to her feet. '*Senhorita*, you are rude and ignorant. I will not listen to such insolence from you!'

Toni bent her head for a moment. 'You provoked any insolence on my behalf, *senhora*,' she said quietly. 'I have no wish to argue with you. It will not solve anything. My leaving here is my concern, and no one else's.'

'Has my – the Conde – asked you to stay?' Laura's voice was shrill.

Toni looked up. 'Actually, yes,' she said, her eyes wide and innocent.

Laura paced about furiously. 'Why?'

'He – he wanted me to take over the position of Francesca's governess!'

'What!' Laura was incredulous. 'You – teaching Francesca!'

'Yes, *senhora*.'

Laura gnawed angrily at her lip. 'And are you staying?'

'I doubt it.'

The older woman's eyes narrowed. 'Why? Have you any reason for refusing?'

Toni heaved a sigh. 'For heaven's sake, *senhora*! Can't we leave this? I don't think it has anything to do with you.'

Laura became even more infuriated. 'It has everything to do with me. I am going to marry Raoul, I shall soon be living at the *castelo*. Do you think I want you here – under my feet?'

'I won't be here, *senhora*.' Toni turned away.

Laura caught her arm, swinging her round to face her again. 'Don't you turn your back on me, *senhorita*. It occurs to me that my – my fiancé's reasons for keeping you here might have a more subtle undertone. And that being so, I think you should know what it is!'

'Oh, leave me alone, *senhora*.' Toni pulled away from her. 'You're all obsessed with intrigue here! All right, all right, I shouldn't have come here, and you can bet I'll leave just as soon as I can!'

Laura looked malevolent, but the door opened then to admit the maid with the tea, and when Francesca and Estevan returned as well, there was no more time for conversation. Francesca looked thoughtfully at Toni when she returned, seeing the girl's flushed cheeks and disturbed eyes, and gave her a warm smile when Toni looked her way. Toni smiled in return, and then gave her attention to her tea. She couldn't eat a thing, however, and excused herself as soon as she was able and went to her room. Once there she flung herself wearily on the bed, wondering why fate had ever thrown her into the turmoil of emotions of the Castelo Estrada.

The next day Toni awoke with a sense of foreboding. Today she must make some definite arrangements about leaving. There was absolutely no reason to wait any longer, and if the Conde returned and found her there, he would imagine she had done as he asked and decided to become Francesca's governess.

Francesca listened to her decision at breakfast with bleak eyes. 'What happened between you and Senhora

Passamentes yesterday?' she asked. 'Has she said anything to make you want to leave?'

Toni buttered a hot roll. 'You might say she precipitated something that would have happened anyway,' she replied truthfully.

'But, Toni, please – don't go!' Francesca bent her head. 'I – I don't want you to go. There's no one here. Grandmother is too old to spend a lot of time with me, and my father – well, sometimes I think he hates me. I remind him too much of – other things!'

Toni bit her lip. 'Francesca, that's not true. About your father hating you, I mean. You know he thinks the world of you. I'm sorry you're alone here – but when your father marries Senhora Passamentes you'll have Estevan to share your days with. Besides, I'm surprised your father doesn't send you to boarding school. I'm sure you'd like that.'

Francesca shrugged. 'Maybe I would, maybe not. I've never wanted to go before when my father suggested it. Besides, then Grandmother would be alone . . .' She looked up. 'I wish I were like you. Free to do as I liked.'

'Oh, Francesca!' Toni felt awful. 'You know it's nothing to do with you. It's just that – well, your father thinks I'm something I'm not.'

'Because of your association with Paul?'

'Partly. And partly something else. Anyway, if I were to stay here I'd be miserable for those reasons.'

Francesca sighed. 'All right, Toni. When – when will you go?'

Toni shook her head. 'I haven't telephoned the airport in Lisbon yet. I might get a flight tomorrow. If I can get a bus from Estrada to Pareira I can take a train straight to Lisbon.'

'*Today?*' said Francesca in dismay.

'Why not? There's no point in prolonging the agony.'

Francesca looked glum. 'At least give me one more day,' she pleaded. 'I mean – that's not so much to ask, is it?'

Toni studied her thoughtfully. 'Well, maybe not. Okay, Francesca, one more day.'

During the morning they swam, and then while Francesca took her siesta Toni packed most of her clothes, surveying her room with a sense of hopelessness that had nothing to do with Francesca.

At dinner the Condessa was talkative. 'Tell me, Janet,' she said gently, 'do you really intend to marry my grandson? I have the strangest feeling that all is not well between you, despite my son's reassurances.'

Toni sighed ruefully. 'You might say all was not well,' she admitted. 'However, our problems need not worry you. Now that I am fully recovered I am thinking of returning to England and we can iron out our difficulties there.'

The Condessa looked distressed. 'To England!' she echoed. 'Oh, but surely, my son told me you were staying on for a while.'

Toni turned bright red. 'The – er – the Conde is very kind,' she stammered. 'But I would prefer to return home all the same.'

'I see.' The Condessa frowned. 'But this is most disappointing. I know the life we lead here is very lonely, and there is little distraction, and yet I had thought you liked it here.'

'Oh, I do! That is – the climate is marvellous. And I love the *castelo* and its environs. But I've spent too long here as it is, and I ought to go back.'

'And when are you thinking of leaving us?'

Toni lifted her shoulders. 'I thought – perhaps – tomorrow!'

'Tomorrow! Oh no, *senhorita*, you cannot leave tomorrow.' The Condessa was most disturbed. 'That is much too soon after your accident. I am sure Doctor Rodrigues said only the day before yesterday, when he examined me, that he would be coming back to see you again next week.'

'Well, I'm afraid that's out of the question,' said Toni firmly. 'Besides, it's not necessary. I'm perfectly capable of seeing my own doctor in England should that be necessary.'

The Condessa sighed. 'You young people are so independent. In my day the elders always knew best.'

'I'm sorry, Condessa, but really, I must go.' Toni felt a sense of urgency assail her. She didn't want to see the Conde again, and she was afraid if he returned she might find herself in deeper waters than she already was.

After dinner was over, Francesca said she was going to bed. Toni was surprised. Usually in the evenings they took a walk together, and as this was her last evening she had thought Francesca would spend it with her. However, thinking Francesca might have taken offence at her abrupt departure plans, she decided to take a last look at the cliffs, and the beach below them.

It was a wonderful evening. The sky was dark velvet inset with jewels, and a sickle moon floated lazily. The scents of the flowers were intoxicating and she felt a sense of regret that in a couple of days she might be back in London, looking out of her bed-sitter window on to the stone yard of the building. There were no flowers there, no romantic castle looking grim, yet inviting, in the moonlight. It would all seem like a dream, a crazy dream, and one which she must forget as soon as possible.

She shivered as she wondered what the Conde would do when he returned and found her gone. He was not a man to take disobedience kindly, and yet what could he do? Once she was back in England, it would not be so easy to trace her, and in any case, what would be the point?

She thought again of the livid scar that had distorted the flesh of his cheek. Its origins seemed shrouded in mystery, and yet she felt sure it had something to do with Paul – and his wife, Elise. It was a guess, of course, but an educated one. There had been so many innuendoes regarding Paul and the Conde's dislike of him, and she wondered whether Paul and the Conde had had a fight. And yet that would hardly account for such a severe wound. Unless they had had knives, which was quite ridiculous.

Thrusting these thoughts aside, she allowed her mind to return to that day in her room when the Conde had seemed to lose control of himself and kissed her. Her skin still burned at the remembrance of that encounter, and she wished she could wipe it from her mind along with all the other things.

She returned to the *castelo* a little after nine, deciding to go straight to bed. The hall was deserted, but she heard sounds in the lounge and thinking it might be the Condessa she walked into the room. She stopped dead when she saw the Conde lounging lazily on a settee, feet outstretched, a cigarette in one hand, a drink in the other, and a newspaper supported on his knees. He had shed his jacket, and in a cream shirt, open at the throat to reveal the beginnings of the dark hairs of his chest, he looked younger, more approachable, and infinitely more dangerous to her peace of mind.

'Shut the door, *senhorita*,' he said indolently, putting his cigarette between his teeth and standing his drink down on a table as he got to his feet.

Toni shivered. 'I don't think we have anything to say to one another, Senhor Conde,' she murmured.

'Yes, we have.' He gave her a sardonic glance, and walking over to her leant behind her and closed the door with his foot. 'Well, well, and you are feeling much better, I hear.'

'Where did you hear that?' asked Toni tightly, wondering why he had arrived so late in the evening.

'From Francesca, of course. I also hear that you and she are becoming very friendly.'

'From Francesca? But how? Oh, she couldn't, she just *couldn't*!'

'Couldn't what? Talk about you? She seems to talk about little else, these days. You have made quite an impression, *senhorita*.'

Toni bent her head, feeling exhausted suddenly. She had thought Francesca liked her, was her friend as well. But obviously she had used today to telephone her father and tell him Toni was planning to leave tomorrow. Why else had he arrived so unexpectedly, and so late at night?

'I don't want to discuss anything with you, *senhor*,' said Toni, feeling the unwanted prick of tears behind her eyes. 'Look, I don't know what you think I am or what you think you can do to me, but I will not stay here, and you can't make me!'

'Oh, I think I can, *senhorita*.'

Toni stared at him. 'How?'

The Conde smiled and poured himself another drink, moving away from her so that her breathing returned to its normal tenor. 'When Paul left here several days ago I gave him a certain sum of money.'

'Oh, yes?'

'Yes. I did this purposely, for two reasons. Firstly – to get rid of him, and secondly – to adjure you to stay.'

'I don't understand you, *senhor*. How could making Paul leave adjure me to stay?'

'Wait, and I will explain, *senhorita*. The money is the key. It would be an easy matter for me to contact the British police and tell them that Paul *stole* that money!'

'What!'

'Yes, it was quite easy to make it appear as though some money had been lifted from my safe, without my knowledge.'

'And why do you think I should care if you do that?' exclaimed Toni angrily.

131

'Because, my dear *senhorita*, you are a sentimentalist at heart. I know a little more about you now. I know you once knew Paul rather well. That you were once almost engaged to him. Almost but not quite, which says something for your mentality, I suppose. At any rate, sufficiently well do you know him that I do not think you would deliberately destroy his reputation.'

'But you would!' she exclaimed incredulously.

'Yes, I would,' he agreed.

'But why? Why?'

'As I once told you, you have a certain – how shall I put it – attraction. You are different from our Portuguese women, as my wife was once different also. And in addition to this, you are a woman without scruples. You attempt to destroy the marriage of a friend of mine; you play the part of a man's fiancée, allowing him to make love to you for money; why then should you object when I tell you that I also find you attractive? Not in the way I would love and respect a woman whom I intended to marry, but merely as a purely physical arrangement, it suits me very well.' Toni couldn't believe her ears. She was horrified. 'Then also you are very conveniently a governess, and as Francesca needs a governess . . .' His voice trailed away.

Toni's fingers were swift and angry, and before he had a chance to stop her she had slapped him violently across his face, uncaring that she struck his scar. He pressed a hand to his cheek, and she felt a moment's compassion, and then he ground out:

'I am sorry if my proposition has come as a shock to you, *senhorita*, and maybe the thought of a man so disfigured making love to you nauseates you, but it is of no matter. I do not care about your childish whims and fancies. You are what you are, and I am not a man to be thwarted!'

'You're crazy!' she gasped, pressing a hand to her stomach. 'Crazy!'

'Oh, no, I think I am perfectly sane,' he remarked, recovering his coolness. 'However, you are entitled to your opinion, of course.'

'But – but you can't do this to me! If – if I were the kind of woman you are making me out to be, why should I care what happens to Paul?' She was trembling and her voice was not quite steady.

He shrugged his broad shoulders. 'Who knows? Nevertheless, I cannot believe you are all bad, and I do not think you would want to make such trouble for a man who is reputedly a friend of yours.'

Toni clenched her fists. 'You expect me to – to – give in to your demands because of Paul!'

'Why not? I did not think it would be so distasteful for you!'

Toni swallowed with difficulty. Her throat felt dry, and she felt as weak as she had done at the start of her period in bed. The Conde della Maria Estrada now replaced his glass on the tray and came purposefully towards her. Toni shook her head, backing away from him, until she came up against the wall by the door, where she stiffened into immobility. The Conde halted a few inches from her, looking down at her with those disturbing dark eyes. His scar gave him a swarthy, piratical appearance, and she quivered with fear.

'Do not be alarmed,' he murmured softly, sliding one hand round her neck, under the heavy weight of her hair which was loose about her shoulders. 'I will not hurt you – Toni.' The way he said her name, with its faintly foreign inflection, turned Toni's bones to water. His nearness melted her resistance, and she was terribly afraid of his power over her.

His grip on her neck tightened suddenly, painfully, and with a groan he jerked her forward, close against him, while his mouth sought the soft warmth of hers. His hands slid round her back, caressing her urgently, arousing emotions she had not known she possessed. Her whole body flamed into vibrant life at his touch, and she wanted desperately to respond.

By an enormous effort of will power she managed to stay immobile, and he became angry at her coldness, his mouth became more demanding, and his arms held her closer so that her body was moulded to his.

'Toni!' he muttered, against her mouth, 'kiss me!'

'No!' Toni struggled violently, managing to get her hands against his chest, pushing him away from her.

Then, as suddenly, she was free, and he had stepped back, his eyes blazing with fury.

'So, senhorita,' he muttered savagely, 'you have gained a temporary reprieve.'

Toni pressed the palms of her hands against her hot cheeks. Her mouth felt bruised, and her whole body ached from the passion of his touch.

'Oh, please,' she whispered despairingly, 'let me go! Don't force me to stay here!'

He turned away to pour himself another drink. 'You

can go,' he said slowly. 'If that is what you want!'

'And – and Paul?'

'Leave Paul to me!'

'You will – incriminate him? Deliberately?'

'As I have said, leave that to me.'

Toni gave an exasperated gasp. '*Senhor*, please. I can't stay. I can't pretend to be Francesca's governess.'

'Why not? You pretended to be Paul's fiancée.'

'That was different.'

'In what way?'

'Oh, it just was. There was no – well, there were no strings attached!'

'And with me there is.'

'You *know* it!' She stifled a sob. 'You are despicable! A disgrace to your family! How can anyone with such authority behave so – so – well, in such a primitive manner?'

He half-smiled sardonically. 'All men are primitive, *senhorita*. We are all alike under the skin. We all have our needs, our desires, however base they may be. That you attract me is not a cause for despair. Many women – I do not boast – would envy you.'

'Then take one of them,' she cried desperately.

'Go to bed, *senhorita*,' he said, turning away. 'It is late, and you are tired. Tomorrow you will see everything differently.'

'No. No, I won't! Oh, please, I want to go home!'

'Home? Where is that? A dreary bedsitter in a back street. Oh, yes, *senhorita*, I know all about you. I know you now have no close ties, no one who will miss you. This is sad, but for me, useful.'

'I'd rather be there – in my dreary bedsitter – than here with you,' she choked.

The sardonic smile deepened. 'Indeed? You do not like the silk sheets on your bed, the sunshine, and the leisure? Well, *senhorita*, we will see. You will find I can be very persuasive.'

Toni believed him. Even now, talking to him like this, the picture he had painted had a seducing quality about it. She wondered how he looked in the early morning, between those silk sheets, with a night's growth of beard on his chin, lean and masculine, making lazy passionate love to her. And then she remembered his contempt and mockery, and the elusive state he was offering her – no, forcing her – to accept!

She shook her head helplessly, fear breaking through everything else, and as tears broke she turned and ran wildly out of the room. Upstairs she slammed the door of her bedroom and was grateful for the key she had never used. She turned it firmly, leaning back against the door for a moment as trembling nausea over-whelmed her. She dashed into the bathroom a moment later and was really sick, violently so, until as she leant against the wall afterwards she felt completely drained of all emotion.

Eventually, she washed and forced herself to return to her bedroom and undress. Then she climbed into bed. There were some pills on the bedside table which Nurse Gonzales had given her in case of emergency, should she ever find it difficult to sleep. With shaking fingers she placed two on her tongue and swallowed them with a mouthful of water. Then she lay and waited for the cotton-wool world of the drug to descend upon her and obliviate all thoughts of any kind from her tired mind.

CHAPTER SEVEN

TONI spent a restless night despite the sleeping pills, and came down to breakfast the next morning wondering how on earth she was expected to act normally. It was like some crazy dream where she was being held prisoner with threats, while fate wove its intricate web about her. She was more than a little frightened; she believed that the Conde Raoul della Maria Estrada meant every word he said, and if she attempted to thwart him Paul would certainly suffer. But was that any real concern of hers? Why should she sacrifice herself for a man she barely liked? And yet it seemed inconceivable in the cold light of morning that the Conde could have been serious in his intentions towards herself. He might desire her presence as a governess; had not the Condessa herself said they were hard to come by in this lonely place? – and maybe his sense of humour was a little perverted. He could not really intend *using* her for anything else – *could he?*

She was startled therefore when she entered the dining-room and found the Conde already seated at the breakfast table. He rose at her entrance, scanning her thoroughly before saying:

'Good morning, *senhorita*, I trust you slept well.'

Toni bit her lip hard, and did not reply. Instead she helped herself to some strong black coffee and seated herself as far away from him as possible.

He half-smiled, and re-seated himself, putting away the newspaper he had been reading, and pouring himself another cup of coffee.

'You look worried, *Toni*,' he murmured, deliberately using her name.

She looked up at him angrily. 'Stop baiting me, Senhor Conde,' she exclaimed. 'You may find this situation amusing, I do not!'

'No? So – then we must do something to improve your opinion, mustn't we? Have you any plans for this morning?'

'None – apart from arranging my journey home,' she retorted.

He lit a cigarette lazily, and then, glancing her way said: 'Oh, you smoke, do you not? Forgive me! Will you have a cigarette?'

Toni shook her head ungraciously, feeling hot resentment overtaking her earlier nervousness. How dare he sit there so calmly, discussing her looks and whether or not she wanted a cigarette, when he must know she was a mass of quivering speculation?

He rose to his feet again, and walked across to the wide windows open to the fresh cooling breeze. Leaning against the casement, he said:

'A pleasant view, is it not? Although I spend much of my time in Lisbon, I find I am always reluctant to return there after a spell at the *castelo*. I am sure you must appreciate this also.'

Toni shut her eyes for a moment, as though in exasperation, and then turned her attention to the newspaper he had flung so carelessly across the table. Although she could not read Portuguese she could look at the pictures, and this she did, ignoring him completely.

With a lazy, yet ruthless, gesture, he walked across and lifted the paper from her unresisting fingers. 'When I speak, Toni, you will listen,' he said decisively. Then he straightened. 'So – now we will make plans for this morning. I suggest we take a drive. Francesca can come with us, and I will show you a little of what it means to be the Conde della Maria Estrada.'

Toni looked helplessly up at him. 'Do I have a choice, *senhor?*'

He smiled. 'No. Go get ready if you have finished your breakfast.'

Toni rose from the table. She contemplated arguing with him, but then her own lack of confidence could not go unnoticed, and she had no intention of allowing him to see how nervous she really was. Instead, she turned and walked out of the room just as Francesca was entering. The girl looked a little distressed when she saw Toni, and Toni stopped a moment.

'So, Francesca,' she said coldly, 'you were not my friend at all, just my keeper!'

Francesca looked at her father. 'That's not true! Papa, what have you told Toni?'

'The truth, that is all, *querida.*'

Francesca gave a helpless shrug of her shoulders. 'But – but what do you mean, then, Toni?'

Toni looked puzzled. 'What do *I* mean?' she echoed. 'When you actually telephoned your father to tell him I was leaving – to enable him to get here in time to stop me!'

'That's not true!' Francesca was obviously hurt. 'Papa!'

Toni looked at Raoul. 'Well, *senhor*? Is that not what you said?'

The Conde drew on his cigarette. 'No. It is not what I said. I said Francesca had told me that you were feeling much better – and so she had. She also told me you were leaving in the morning – on my arrival here. It was all presumption on your behalf that put two and two together and made five!'

Toni heaved a heavy sigh. 'I see. I'm sorry, Francesca. I seem to have made another mistake.'

Francesca looked anxious. 'That is all right, Toni. But – but you *are* staying, aren't you? You will stay and be my governess, won't you?'

Toni shook her head. 'You had better ask your father that question too, Francesca. Your answers seem to be more understanding than mine.' And with that she left the room.

In her own room she sat on the bed wondering how on earth she had allowed herself to get into this situation. She had to leave – she *must* leave, but how could she do so without causing Paul a great deal of trouble. And yet would the Conde really implicate his own nephew? It was a gamble she was not yet prepared to take. She would have to stay on at the *castelo*, at least temporarily, and play the cards as she was dealt them. One thing was certain, the Conde della Maria Estrada would not find her a willing victim.

She changed into a flared linen skirt and a pink candystripe blouse that complemented the tan she was acquiring. Then with sandals on her feet she again went downstairs. The Conde and Francesca were awaiting her in the hall, and she managed to smile quite naturally at Francesca as they went out into the courtyard. They climbed into an open tourer, all three together in the front, with Francesca in the middle, and drove away east into the rising sun.

For all Toni's apprehensions, it turned out to be a wonderful and interesting day. They drove to the scorching, arid slopes above the Douro, and Toni saw the grapes ripening in the burning heat of the sun. At last she was beginning to learn a little about the wine that gave Portugal its fame. Interested in the object of their expedition, for a while she forgot to be antagonistic towards Raoul della Maria Estrada and discovered instead that he could talk with ease about so many things, most particularly his vineyards and his estate. Until then she had never looked for this intelligent mind behind his façade of indolence which she had guessed all along was there. She had been so busy arguing with him that she had almost forgotten his part in the family business, that of supervising the many aspects of the estates and its environs.

It was hot in the valley of the upper Douro, and Toni found a piece of string and tied up her hair off her neck. Francesca's plait became heavy, too, and only the Conde in his thin silk shirt, almost open to his waist, seemed unaffected by the sun. Seeing him like this, muscular and tanned, lazy and relaxed, disturbed Toni more than his continual baiting, and she was glad Francesca's presence forestalled any overtures on his part.

After lunch, which they ate at the home of Vasco Braganca, the manager of the vineyard, they drove nearer to the coast again, where in the chalk cliffs, caves provided the natural fermenting cellars for the wine. Here there were galleries with rows of bottles and vats, and Toni wandered, amazed at the intricacies of the timbered workrooms.

'You see,' said the Conde, close beside her, 'it is no easy matter to produce a perfect wine. The grapes must be picked at the exact moment of ripening. This differs according to exposure and altitude; sometimes one vineyard is completely gathered in before another higher placed vineyard is quite ready. It is a complicated business, but when the grapes are picked, and the wine is beginning its fermentaton, it is a time for rejoicing and the pickers are the most excited of all!'

'Dancing on the grapes,' said Toni, looking up at him a smile hovering about her lips.

'Exactly. It is done – still – and there is much singing and dancing, and merrymaking. You see, my people are not so downtrodden as you would have me believe!'

'I didn't say they were downtrodden,' exclaimed Toni.

'No?' he smiled. 'Perhaps not. At any rate, we will not argue today, no?'

'No,' she agreed.

Later they drove into Oporto, and in the harbour they saw the picturesque *rabelos* which the Conde told Toni were used for transporting the barrels of wine downstream from the vineyards.

'It is quite a journey,' he said, smiling. 'The craft are not large, and in the rapid waters of the Douro which lap against the rocky walls of the cliffs, it can be a very dangerous trip.'

'Have you made the trip, *senhor*?' asked Toni politely.

'Many times,' said the Conde patiently. 'I am sorry to disappoint you. You probably thought I would never attempt anything so foolhardy. But you are wrong, *senhorita*, as you will discover!'

It was late when they arrived back at the *castelo*. They had eaten in Oporto, and both Toni and Francesca felt pleasantly tired.

'Tomorrow we will attend a bullfight,' said the Conde, as they entered the hall of the *castelo*. 'You would like that, Toni?'

Toni flushed and looked at Francesca. 'Ought we not to – to commence these lessons, *senhor*?' she asked.

Francesca looked horrified, and the Conde placed a hand gently on her head. 'No, not tomorrow, Francesca. While I am free, we will take advantage of it – *sim*?'

Francesca nodded furiously, and Toni shrugged. 'As you wish, *senhor*.'

'And you, *senhorita*, do you not find that sightseeing can be enjoyable, also?' He frowned. 'I had thought you enjoyed yourself today.'

'I do – I did!' Toni sighed. 'Excuse me now, *senhor*. I am tired. I want to retire.'

'Very well.' The Conde walked to the door of the lounge. 'I will see you both in the morning.'

Taking this as a dismissal of herself too, Francesca kissed her father's cheek, and accompanied Toni up the staircase. On the first landing where the corridor branched to Toni's room, Francesca said:

'You did enjoy yourself today, didn't you, Toni?' rather wistfully.

Tony could not deny this. 'Of course I did. It's been a wonderful day.'

'And tomorrow – you will come with us tomorrow?'

'I don't have any choice,' replied Toni a trifle dryly, and then, repenting, she continued: 'My position here is so nebulous, Francesca. Try to understand how I feel.'

Francesca sighed. 'You do believe that I did not – so to speak – betray you to my father, don't you?'

Toni studied the young girl. 'Nevertheless, it was strange that the Conde should return at such an unexpected moment.'

Francesca lifted her shoulders. 'Not really, Toni,' she said with a resigned sigh. 'My grandmother innocently told my father you were planning to leave. He was not in Lisbon, you understand, but staying with some friends in Coimbra before returning here. My grandmother's information gave him the opportunity to return here yesterday.'

'I see.'

'When my father is away he often telephones my grandmother to enquire about her health.'

Toni nodded. 'How did you find all this out?'

'Papa told me this morning, while you were changing. I told him I was very angry with him for allowing you to think I had deliberately gone behind your back to tell him you were leaving. On the contrary, I was very distressed about it all. But I would not have forced you to stay.'

'No, I see that now, Francesca. I'm sorry. I misjudged you.'

Francesca squeezed her arm. 'Nevertheless, I am glad you are staying, Toni.'

In the next few days the Conde went out of his way to disarm Toni. He and Francesca took her on several expeditions, exploring the countryside around the *castelo* more widely than she had done with Francesca alone, and seeing a little of the country's culture. They attended a bullfight, a much more humane affair than the Spanish equivalent, where the bull is not slaughtered in the ring. They spent an evening at a folk music festival in Oporto, listening to the sad, plaintive music of the *fado*. They visited museums and art galleries, and Toni was struck anew by the immense store of knowledge the Conde could display so carelessly. It was a calm and peaceful time, with no undercurrents to mar their relationship, and Toni almost began to believe that her earlier conversations with the Conde had never occurred. It didn't seem possible that he could possibly find anything of interest in her when he held an *open sesame* to the homes of so many beautiful women.

It was towards the end of the week that Laura Passamentes put in an appearance. She arrived one afternoon while Francesca and Toni were on the beach, and when they returned windswept and sunburnt from the sands they found her seated with the Conde in the lounge, drinking tea from the bone china tea service while the Conde lay lazily in a chair, a glass of whisky and water hanging carelessly from his fingers.

She frowned when she saw Toni, and gave the Conde a speculative glance. 'So, *senhorita*,' she said, 'you are still here.'

Toni nodded. 'As you can see,' she conceded slowly. Francesca hunched her shoulders, and said:

'How are you, Tia Laura?' politely.

'Very well, thank you, Francesca,' replied Laura smoothly, looking up again at the Conde who had risen at their entrance. 'Come and sit beside me and tell me what you have been doing with yourself. Estevan and I have been quite desolated. Raoul has been here a week already and he has not found time to come and visit with us.'

Francesca flushed, and Toni made for the door again just as the Condessa arrived. 'You are not leaving, are you, my dear?' she exclaimed, touching her arm gently. 'I was just coming to have tea with Laura. You must stay and have some with us, eh, Raoul?'

The Conde gave a slight movement of his shoulders. 'Of course, *mae*, if that is what you wish.'

Toni looked at him exasperatedly. 'I'd rather not, *senhor*,' she said quietly.

His thick lashes veiled his eyes. 'But you will,' he murmured, and for the first time for days Toni felt the faint stirrings of apprehension.

'All right, *senhor*.' Toni's voice was tight, and she moved back to the couch and sat where he indicated.

Laura dominated the conversation. She seemed to find the greatest enjoyment in catechizing Francesca, and Toni thought that maybe this was the only way she got candid answers to her sometimes personal questions. After all, hadn't she herself already had a sample of the Senhora's inquisition?

'And what have you been doing these last few days?' Laura was asking Francesca now. 'Did you know there was a folk music festival in Oporto?'

'Oh yes!' Francesca was enthusiastic and unthinking because of it. 'We've been there!'

'You've been?' Laura's eyes turned to Raoul. 'You went to the festival, *querido*?'

The Conde looked a little bored. 'Yes, Laura, we went to the festival. It was very good.'

'And you did not ask me also?' Laura looked disturbed.

'I did not think it would interest you,' returned the Conde smoothly. 'What have you been doing with yourself?'

'Very little, and you must know I love folk music. You took Francesca – and your mother?'

The Condessa shook her head. 'What would I want with folk festivals, Laura? No, Raoul took Francesca and Senhorita West."

'Senhorita *West*?' Laura gasped.

Raoul gave her a warning look. 'Yes, Laura, Senhorita West.'

'I see.' Laura cast a malevolent glance in Toni's direction. 'And did you enjoy it, *senhorita*?'

'Very much, thank you.'

Laura replaced her cup in its saucer. 'And when do you plan to leave, *senhorita*?'

Toni lifted her shoulders. 'I don't know—'

'The Senhorita is to stay indefinitely,' said Francesca excitedly. 'She is going to be my governess!'

'This is so, Raoul?' Laura was astounded.

'Yes.' The Conde was abrupt. 'But this can be of no interest to you, Laura. Come, I will show you the painting I bought in Coimbra ten days ago. It is a Miró, and should appeal to you.'

'But this is of interest to me, *caro*,' insisted Laura. 'After all, your mother must think it strange that the Senhorita should be able to give up her job in England without giving notice.'

Raoul gave her a darkening look. 'It is not your affair, Laura. If – if the Senhorita chooses to stay here, then we are all delighted, are we not? Surely you can have no objections to Francesca acquiring a governess to whom she has so obviously taken?'

Laura frowned. 'It is a little unorthodox, that is all. Do you not think so, dear Condessa?'

The old Condessa seemed unmoved by this exchange and seemed totally intent on helping herself to a cup of tea. 'Whatever Janet decides I shall be entirely in agreement,' she said, absently studying the spoon in her hand. 'Did I put sugar in my tea, or did I not? You see, Laura, you have confused me!'

Laura rose impatiently to her feet. 'I will see the Miró, Raoul,' she said shortly, and walked to the door without another word.

After they had gone Toni relaxed and lay back

against the soft upholstery. Francesca gave her a conspiratorial smile, but Toni was too engrossed with her own thoughts to pay much attention to the younger girl. With the Conde's peremptory command had returned all her misgivings, and she wondered, with a sense of dismay, how much longer he intended to stay at the *castelo*.

The following morning Toni rose earlier than usual. She had slept badly again and there were dark rings round her eyes. She thought a bathe in the warm waters of the Atlantic might banish the faint stirrings of a headache that probed the back of her mind, so she donned a bathing suit and her beach dress and after collecting a towel made her way down to the beach. The sand was already warming in the heat of the new day, but it was still cool enough to cause her to shiver as she ran to plunge into the waves. She swam, forcing her mind to remain blank, floating on her back with her hair around her in the water like seaweed. Then she swam back to the shallows and walked up the sand wringing the water out of her hair.

She stopped short at the sight of the Conde lounging lazily on the sands near her beach dress and towel and sandals. Then, with slower steps, she approached him.

'Good morning, *senhor*,' she said politely. 'I did not expect to find you here.'

'Perhaps not; and perhaps it would be as well if you were to call me Raoul when we are alone. I do not care for you to be so formal.'

'I prefer formality, *senhor*,' replied Toni deliberately,

bending to lift her towel.

He caught her wrist in a vice-like grip, pulling her down beside him so that she overbalanced and fell in the sand. Then he leant over her, pinning her to the sand with both hands, looking down at her with eyes that had darkened with passion. Toni struggled to free herself, and he said:

'Why do you persistently fight me? For once, at least, submit!'

Toni turned her head from side to side. 'I hate you, I hate you!'

'What is it you hate?' he exclaimed harshly, 'the man – or the scar?'

Toni's eyes rested on the scar for a moment. Curiously, she realized that she had grown accustomed to its presence. It did not disturb her except in a strangely vulnerable way. She stopped struggling.

'Your scar doesn't bother me,' she said breathlessly, only aware of him: his warmth and passion, the heavy muscularity of his body, and most of all his eyes and mouth. She wanted him to kiss her, she realized again. As before, his overwhelming attraction had thrust her own inhibitions aside.

'You do not think perhaps that my mind is distorted because my face is distorted also,' he murmured huskily, caressing the nape of her neck with one hand.

'Raoul—' she groaned, unable to prevent herself, and with a half-triumphant exclamation he bent his head and parted her lips with his mouth.

'So,' he murmured, burying his face in her neck, 'you do not hate me after all, *cara*.'

It was very quiet on the beach, only the early morning cries of the sea-birds wheeling overhead, and the gentle thunder of the waves upon the rocks to break the stillness. Toni felt a growing feeling of inertia overtaking her, as he continued to kiss her with persistent passion. As she had once imagined in her foolishness, he was expert at getting what he wanted, and just now he wanted her. The awful danger was that she was beginning to want him, too, and that was something she had never before experienced. She had never felt this aching heightening of her senses so that she longed to hold him even closer until their bodies were moulded together.

With a superhuman effort, she managed to take him by surprise, wriggling out of his grasp when he least expected it, scrambling to her feet with panic-stricken movements. Leaving her beach dress and towel where they lay, she ran swiftly across the sand, unheeding of his angry command for her to return.

Her legs would hardly carry her up the steep rocky steps. Every minute she expected to hear him behind her, preventing her escape, taking her back and making rough and violent love to her. But there was no sound, and when she reached the top of the steps she looked back and saw him standing with his back to her in the same spot as she had left her clothes.

She halted uncertainly, a shaking, trembling clutch of nerves. What was he thinking? What terrible revenge might he be planning to take? She shivered, and turning began to walk slowly towards the *castelo*. It hardly seemed possible that in so few weeks her whole life could have been so altered. Life in England, the bed-sitter, the shock of her parents' death, even Paul himself all seemed a lifetime away. All she could remember was this – this kind of mental agony that the Conde was making her suffer. Whether or not he was conscious of it, his enforced denial of her physical possession was more tortuous than actual submission might have been.

She reached her room without encountering anyone and took a shower to wash the sand from her hair and her body. As she dried herself and dressed in slim slacks and a sleeveless sweater she wondered why she didn't just pack up and go. She had stayed, she had discovered the Conde could be a charming and intelligent companion, she had given herself time to recover completely from the accident, and most important of all she had given Paul another week in which the Conde ought to have reported his so-called theft if indeed that was what he had intended to do. It was too long now for him not to have discovered the discrepancy; at least, surely that would be the judgment of the police if they were called.

She sighed. So why didn't she go? She could easily escape; she was not supervised, and it would not be difficult to leave without being noticed for some time. *So why didn't she?*

Her brain tossed the question back and forth insistently, as she rubbed her hair dry and fastened it with elastic bands. There was only one answer, of course, as she had known all along. She didn't want to leave any more. She might fight the Conde, with every ounce of her being, she might refuse his ultimate possession of her, and yet, deep down, that was what she wanted. But not on his terms, *not on his terms*! He was a fine man, a wonderful man, cruel and ruthless, when there was something he particularly wanted, and yet basically honest; a man it was fatally easy to love. *To love*! She stared at her reflection, a horrified expession dawning in her eyes. That was the truth, wasn't it? No matter what he had done, how he had treated her, what manner of punishment he might mete out to her, she was *in love* with him.

She turned away, refusing to look into her own eyes and see the truth. It couldn't be true! It *mustn't* be true! She sank down on to the edge of the bed, the brush dropping heedlessly from her fingers. It was true, it *was*! She was in love with a man who thought she was easy game, someone to have an affair with, a woman who was cheap! How he would laugh if he ever found out. Or maybe he already had. Maybe her urgent response to his lovemaking had given her away. Maybe even now he was laughing to himself. How easy it would be for him to force her to submit if he knew she had no resistance against him! She shivered, and bending, picked the brush from the floor. She replaced it on the dressing table, avoiding her eyes, and walking to the window. The heat of the day was strengthening. How beautiful was the vista of sea and shoreline. It was a fairytale castle, but she was no fairytale princess. Rather more like a helpless mouse caught in the net of a jungle beast, who wanted to play with its prey before destroying it.

CHAPTER EIGHT

IT was late before she went down for breakfast, but Francesca was still at the table, staring moodily into space, her eyes thoughtful. She looked up when Toni entered, and said:

'You're late! I thought you weren't going to bother to come at all.'

Toni seated herself beside the percolator. 'I'm sorry, honey. I – I went down to the beach. I had a swim before breakfast, and then I had to shower before getting dressed.'

'Oh – I see.' Francesca heaved a sigh. 'Did you know my father was leaving this morning?'

Toni looked astonished. 'No – I mean – has he *left*?'

'Yes. I didn't see him, but he has gone. Maria said he didn't have any breakfast at all.'

'I see.' Toni swallowed hard. 'Where – where has he gone?'

'Back to Lisbon, I believe.' Francesca traced a pattern on the cloth. 'I wish he'd told me he was leaving.'

Toni sensed the girl's disappointment, and got up and came round to her. 'Never mind, I guess he must have had something urgent on his mind.'

'Do you think so?' Francesca looked up at Toni. 'I cannot help but associate Laura's visit yesterday with his subsequent departure.'

Toni's heart plunged. 'Why?'

'I don't know. Maybe she said something. Certainly she objected to his being here with you around. Perhaps she's jealous.'

'That would be ridiculous,' exclaimed Toni shortly.

'Why? What is ridiculous about it? I've thought for some time that my father enjoyed your company. Hasn't this past week proved it to you?'

'This past week has been a week out of time,' said Toni, sighing herself now. 'You've no idea what kind of an opinion your father has of me!'

Francesca looked impatient. 'You're imagining things! If you had known my father as long as I have you would realize that his treatment of you these past days has been more like that of a − − an admirer than anything else! I think he finds you amusing. You're not like Laura, and the other women who try to attract him. In fact, I'm sure you go out of your way to annoy him, and maybe this is the secret of your attraction.'

'For heaven's sake, Francesca!' Toni felt exasperated. 'Let's drop it, shall we? You haven't the faintest idea what you're talking about. You sound as though you've been listening to petty gossip in the servants' quarters. Those words you've just spoken sound exactly like the sort of thing you read in women's magazines!' She smiled, trying to distract Francesca's trend of conversation.

Francesca shrugged and rose to her feet. 'Well, anyway, he left instructions that we should start lessons, so we might as well.'

Toni's eyes widened. 'You actually *want* to start lessons!'

Francesca looked sulky. 'Well, if we do, at least you won't have time to brood about leaving,' she retorted.

Toni thought there might be some truth in that. It would help to have something to do to take her mind from her personal problems.

'All right,' she said. 'Come on, we might as well begin.'

For all that Francesca was only thirteen she was already well advanced in her studies towards the Portuguese equivalent of the 'O' level. Toni doubted her own capacity for being able to teach her much. It was merely necessary to study her books and advise her on the exercises she should concentrate on. She was particularly good at English, and Francesca confided that her father had said she might attend an English university. She was an apt pupil and she and Toni had many interesting conversations and debates on various sociological subjects. She was well read and could quote Shakespeare and Dickens, as well as many British poets. She loved poetry, and as this had always been Toni's favourite subject they spent hours reading from an old edition of the works of William Wordsworth. So many of the Lakeland poets seemed, to Toni, to express the very essence of a love of nature, and here, among such wild and beautiful scenery, it was not difficult to realize how they gained their inspiration. If the knowledge that one day the Conde would return disturbed her, it was quickly dispelled during the daylight hours when she had the Conde's daughter as her companion. Francesca was so much like her father, with his capacity for learning and expressing herself. She also had his sense of humour, and Toni was almost content.

It was only at night, when the moon hung low over the *castelo* walls, and the sky was a velvet background for the jewel-like stars that she felt the stirrings of love and desire, arousing an awareness of herself and of the needs of her own body and mind. She remembered every tiny detail about the Conde della Maria Estrada: the thick smoothness of his hair, the long luxuriant length of his lashes, the tanned, artistic, yet hard slenderness of his hands, which could arouse her to such ecstatic delight in submission, and the livid scar which seemed, despite his protestations, to have influenced him in some strange way.

Many times she sat by her window, listening to the roar of the sea, and the gentle murmurings of the night animals, wondering where he was, and what he was doing, and when he would come back to claim her, utterly. The old Condessa accepted her presence without question, and Toni could only assume that she took little interest in the affairs of the *castelo*, so long as they remained smooth. Francesca saw more of the Condessa than anyone, as from time to time she was confined to her bed by the doctor, and then Francesca went and drank tea with her, and told her what they were doing.

One hot afternoon, about two weeks after the Conde had left for Lisbon, the Condessa took Francesca out for a drive with her. They invited Toni to join them, but she refused, saying she wanted to wash her hair and catch up on some small mending repairs. It was late afternoon before they left as the Condessa always had a siesta after lunch.

After they had gone, Toni washed her hair, and collecting her mending made her way down to the arbour behind the *castelo*, where she could sit in the shade of a huge magnolia tree. It was peaceful there, the sun filtering through the branches on to her bent head. She sewed for a while and then sat combing her hair which was drying in the heat of the air. She did not hear a car arrive at the *castelo* and so she was surprised when she heard voices and footsteps approaching along the paved path leading the arbour. She glanced round in time to see Laura Passamentes approaching accompanied by Luisa, the housekeeper. They were speaking Portuguese, but Toni gathered that Luisa was showing Laura where she was.

When Laura saw her, she dismissed Luisa with a wave of her hand and came through the trellised arch to join Toni.

'So, *senhorita*,' she said coldly, 'you are still here. And alone, I believe. Luisa tells me that the Condessa and Francesca are out for a drive.'

'That is correct, *senhora*,' replied Toni politely, putting aside her comb. 'Are you well?'

'Perfectly, *senhorita*,' replied Laura shortly.

'Well, won't you sit down?' asked Toni, indicating the seat beside her.

'No. I have no wish to sit with *you*, *senhorita*,' retorted Laura rudely.

Toni wet her lips with her tongue. 'But you came here – you asked Luisa to show you the way here – so that you could see me, *senhora*.'

'I did, I agree. But not perhaps for the reasons you believe.'

Toni sighed. 'What reasons?'

Laura shrugged. She was wearing a dark blue dress which moulded her body, and Toni thought she had never looked so beautiful, or so aristocratic.

'When I arrived, it was with the intention of procuring a moment alone with you, 'Senhorita Morley,' said Laura, surprisingly. 'However, when I found the Condessa and Francesca were not at home. I could not have been more pleased. Not because I do not wish to see the Condessa, who is a dear and close friend of mine, or Francesca either, although of late she has shown a little rudeness in my presence, but simply because it gives me the opportunity to see you without fear of being overheard.'

Toni stiffened. '*Senhora*,' she said, trying to keep her voice steady, 'this is the third time we have – how shall I put it – had words over the Conde, for I am sure that is what you are here to discuss, and quite frankly, I am sick and tired of it. I do not wish to be rude, *senhora*, but if you have any complaints about my presence here, you should take them up with the Conde himself, not me!'

'Do not be insolent, *senhorita*,' exclaimed Laura, taken aback. 'You are right, of course, I do wish to speak with you concerning Raoul, and I have no intention of discussing this particular, and painful, matter with him.'

'*Senhora*,' began Toni wearily, 'there's nothing more to be said. . . .'

'On the contrary, there is a great deal to be said,' contradicted Laura, becoming annoyed. 'For example, why, if you do not wish to stay here, do you stay?'

'Did I say I didn't wish to stay here?'

'Not today, no. But that other time we spoke together.'

Toni bit her lip. 'I don't think I need to discuss my reasons with you, *senhora*.'

'Oh, no? Then let me tell you, *senhorita*, shall I? The reason you stay here is because you are in love with the Conde!'

'*Senhora!*' Toni was horrified.

'Can you deny it? No, you cannot.' Laura paced about angrily. 'I have known it for some time, of course. But it also occurred to me that you might have some idea that by staying here – that by Raoul *allowing* you to stay here – you are in some way an attraction for him!' Laura gave a short laugh. 'How stupid you are, *senhorita*, to imagine that the Conde Raoul Felipe Vincente della Maria Estrada might be interested in you! Oh, you are not unattractive, in a purely – peasant – way—'

'How dare you!' Toni was speechless.

'—and it is possible that given enough encouragement Raoul might amuse himself by playing with you a little, but never – never for one moment – imagine that it is anything more than that!'

Toni groped for words. 'What gives you the right to come here and speak to me like this? You are not even engaged to him!'

Laura tossed her head. 'A mere formality, I can

161

assure you. We do not rush carelessly into things here as you do in your country, making mistakes and paying for them with a lifetime of misery!' She halted. 'Estelle – the Senhora de Calle, that is – warned me about you! Told me what a snake in the grass you might be!'

Toni got unsteadily to her feet. 'Will you go away?' she said weakly. 'I don't have to listen to this kind of talk – from you!'

'Sit down,' and as Toni protested, Laura almost shouted the words: 'Sit down, *senhorita*.'

Astonishment vied with disbelief on Toni's face as she sank back into her seat. Then Laura put her hands on her hips, studying her insolently.

'Now, *senhorita*, I will tell you something that you might find – interesting.'

'I don't want to listen!' Toni put her hands over her ears, but she could still hear Laura's raised voice.

'Haven't you ever wondered why Paul is not welcome here, *senhorita*? You must have done! And do not deny that you are curious about Raoul's dreadful scar!'

'It's not dreadful!' The words were wrung from Toni's lips.

'It is – it is nauseating!' exclaimed Laura furiously. 'But it is of no matter. When we are married I shall persuade him to have plastic surgery to remove it.'

Toni turned away. Already Laura was planning to change Raoul, even before they were positively engaged to be married. What would his life be like if she actually married him?

Then she chided herself for caring. When had he ever cared about her!

'So,' continued Laura relentlessly, 'I will tell you. Paul – your so-called friend and erstwhile so-called fiancé – was having an affair with Elise, Raoul's wife!'

'What!' Toni at last looked at her in amazement. 'But – but ten years ago – Elise had a daughter of three!'

'That is so. Ten years ago she was twenty-five – Paul was a mere twenty, but that did not stop them! Elise's marriage to Raoul was never a success – Paul came here, when Raoul's father died, and they were immediately attracted. Elise was bored – Raoul was away a lot. It is a lonely place. Paul was young – and handsome, I suppose – and Elise was not the kind of woman to care who she hurt in the process!'

Toni shook her head disbelievingly. So that was why Raoul hated Paul, and with good reason. But that still did not explain the scar.

'This is not my affair, *senhora*,' she said dully. 'You are disclosing family matters to a comparative stranger!'

'Yes, I am. And with good reason! You must be made to see how stupid you are being!' She stamped her foot in impatience. 'But wait – I have not finished yet. There is more. I must tell you about the day Elise was killed!'

Toni bent her head, despising herself for wanting to know the truth when it could never help her in any way. 'Don't go on,' she pleaded. 'I don't want to know!'

'Of course you do, *senhorita*. You are timid, that is all, afraid perhaps of what you might hear!'

'Maybe I am,' said Toni, looking at her. 'But at least I am honest. I do not pretend to be something I am not!'

Laura gasped. 'You! You dare to say that to me when you are continually living a life of pretence! Does the Condessa yet know you are not Paul's fiancée?'

Toni lifted her shoulders. 'All right, I did pretend to be Paul's fiancée, but quite innocently, I can assure you. At that time I had no idea of his reasons for bringing me here.'

'You expect me to believe that? Did you not yourself expect to get a cut of whatever Paul managed to inveigle out of his grandmother!'

Toni sprang to her feet. 'You – you – bitch!' she exclaimed.

'Do not dare to call me names, *senhorita*,' shouted Laura hysterically, 'or I may call you a few you will not like to hear! Much more descriptive words than that which you use!'

'Well, you are!' exclaimed Toni, her cheeks burning. 'I'm sure Raoul has no idea of the creature you really are!'

'Don't speak Raoul's name so carelessly, *senhorita*. It is not yours to use. He is the Conde della Maria Estrada, and don't you ever forget it.'

'How could I?' exclaimed Toni, tears burning her eyes now.

'Indeed, how could anyone forget a man who is so unique!' Laura calmed down. 'Nevertheless, there is one more thing you should know. The night Elise was killed she was leaving Raoul – to go to Paul in London. Whether Paul actually intended this was what she should do, I do not know, for he never had any money of his own. But he had acted without considering the temperamental nature of a woman like Elise, who after a row with Raoul left here in a blazing temper. It is not difficult to imagine her crashing the car – she was never an expert driver – but when she was killed, it had a destroying effect on Raoul for a while.' Laura made an eloquent gesture with her hands. 'By that, I do not mean he went to pieces entirely. After all, he did not love her—'

'She was the mother of his child,' Toni reminded her quietly, seeing the angry flush rise again in Laura's cheeks.

'A marriage of convenience, nothing more,' retorted Laura. 'However, for a time Raoul seemed restless, he would not settle to anything, and it was then he took up motor racing. You must have noticed his taste in fast cars; he had always driven fast, but expertly. It was not surprising, therefore, that he chose that way in which to assuage his – grief, for want of a better word.'

'I see. And I suppose he must have crashed.'

'Many times,' agreed Laura impatiently. 'Racing drivers are accustomed to crashing. It was only when the final crash occurred, and he almost lost his life, that it seemed to dawn on him that he still had a daughter and a life of his own.'

'I still don't see what this has to do with me,' said Toni, sighing.

'Don't you? Well, I will explain further. You are a

little like Elise yourself. She was fair also, and blue-eyed—'

'My eyes are not blue, they are green,' said Toni tautly.

'So? It is of no matter. That you are sufficiently like her is enough. Also, you came here with Paul – you were Paul's friend, and as such a reminder of bitter memories. It occurred to me that Raoul might find it amusing to use you to assuage his bitterness towards Paul and Elise!'

Toni felt her throat was dry, and her tongue seemed glued to the roof of her mouth. With every succeeding sentence Laura seemed to be slowly destroying all the life and hope inside her. She would not have believed anyone could emanate such cruelty, even though Laura might not be aware of the whole extent of the pain she was inflicting.

Was it possible that that was the reason the Conde had kept her here? Could he be using her to rid himself at last of his bitterness towards Elise? And was it possible that he might also be destroying Paul by using the money as his weapon? Even now, Paul could be in prison for an offence he did not commit. She would never know, here, isolated from all British newspapers. After all, the Conde had been away some considerable time. What was he doing? Was he really only working? Or was there some deeper, hidden reason for his sudden departure? And was she waiting here for his return, like some meek creature, without any spine or spunk, when he was really only laughing at her? How stupidly had she imagined there conceivably might be some kinder reason!

Laura at last seemed to have exhausted herself and was walking to the trellised arch that led out of the arbour.

'I can see I have at last pierced your sensibilities,' she said, with some satisfaction. 'I will go before the good Condessa returns and insists that I stay for dinner. I have no desire to sit at the table with you, *senhorita*.'

Toni was too numb to answer her, and without another word Laura walked away. After she had gone, Toni lifted her sewing and looked at it unseeingly. She felt sick and shaky, and wished with all her heart she had accompanied the Condessa and Francesca on their journey. Then she would have heard none of this, but would she have been any happier? Sooner or later, Laura would have found a way to let her know the truth about Paul, and Elise, and the Conde, and the longer she waited the harder it would get. Yet she doubted that anything could be harder than Laura's words today. Such small defences that she had had been destroyed with relentless persistence, and now she was left without hope. What malevolence Laura possessed, though, to be able to come and speak so vitriolically without appearing to turn a hair! A woman like that could never love a man like Raoul, could never give him the warmth and passion and response that Toni had known he demanded. For all his faults he was a man of flesh and blood, while Laura was merely obsessed with affluence and the power of being the Condessa della Maria Estrada.

She could see Laura's point, of course, it was simple.

The Conde, because of Paul, had lost his wife and been scarred for life, and not only physically. He must have been so embittered by it all that he chose any way to assuage that bitterness. That she had had very little to do with it was her own misfortune. If she had never agreed to Paul's crazy plan, she would never have met the Conde, never have involved herself in something so complicated. She had no one but herself to blame.

By the time the Condessa and Francesca returned from their drive she had made up her mind what she intended to do. She would leave, tonight, without telling anyone. She could leave a note for Francesca to find and be many miles away before her presence was missed from the Castelo Estrada. It was no use risking telling Francesca; although she had not told the Conde that other time, there was no reason to suppose she would still feel the same.

She made a pretence of eating dinner with the Condessa and Francesca and then excused herself on the grounds of having a headache. She accepted their sympathy, feeling guilty that she should be intending to leave so tardily, but then hardening her heart when she recalled the reasons behind her enforced employment as Francesca's governess. In her room she packed her belongings with a sense of misery she had not realized anyone could suffer. Then she dressed in slacks and a sweater, leaving her jacket lying on top of her cases. She sat down to wait for the rest of the household to retire, a pen and paper on her knees as she tried to think of something to say to Francesca. In the end she merely wrote that she was leaving, not to try and stop her, and that she would write more fully when she reached London. Then she wrote Francesca's name on the envelope and put it beside her cases.

It seemed ages before the *castelo* became silent. She had never before heard all the sounds of the night with such clarity. Several times she stiffened when she thought she heard footsteps coming her way, but after a while all was quiet. The *castelo* had settled down for the night.

She glanced at her watch. It was a little after midnight, seven hours before the kitchen staff came on duty and at least eight hours before Francesca would find the note.

Opening her door, she stood for a moment listening, making certain that there was no sound, then she lifted her cases and her jacket, putting the envelope addressed to Francesca in her pocket. She crept along the corridor, past the Condessa's bedroom, and down the stairs. It was strange and eerie without any lights, and she had to trust to her own surefootedness not to lose her way. In the hall, a low lamp was burning on an occasional table, and she put the letter on the copper dish beside it. Then she opened the door leading into the corridor which in turn led to the outer door of the building.

The courtyard was deserted, only a dog barking in one of the out-houses seemed capable of hearing her. Keeping in the shadows, just in case, she made her way to the garages, housed near the Great Hall. She knew that the chauffeur did not bother to lock either the garages or the cars, and it would not be difficult to take one.

The garage door presented more of a problem. It creaked on its hinges, and she froze into immobility at the unexpected sound. But apart from an increased spasm of barking from the dog, there was no other movement. There was the huge limousine used by the Condessa on her infrequent jaunts into the country, and there was the dusty Landrover used by one of the servants when stores were needed from the shops in Pareira. As borrowing any kind of vehicle without the owner's permission was alien to her nature Toni decided on the Landrover as being the least important of the two. The keys hung loosely in the ignition, and dumping her cases in the back, she climbed in. Starting the motor caused yet another problem. The engine was temperamental and took several attempts at revving to bring it into operation, and Toni was positively shaking with nerves as she drove shakily across the drawbridge and out on to the main courtyard before the *castelo*.

Getting her bearings, she turned east towards Pareira. Estrada itself was only a fishing village and of no use to her. Besides, she did not want to draw attention to herself, and in Pareira she could be anonymous.

The moon illuminated the road, but even so she felt a little frightened. She had never driven at night before, indeed she had not driven at all since her parents' car crash. She wondered what she would do if the Landrover broke down, or if someone forced her to stop. Such thoughts were unpleasant and with an effort she tried to concentrate on other things. Things back in London, for example. It would be nice to see her bed-sitter again, which her landlady was keeping for her at a nominal fee. Then she would meet her friends again, girls who lived in the same building. Even the agency might be pleased to see her.

Only her aching heart warned her that it would not be that easy. Not easy at all to forget Estrada, the *castelo*, the Condessa, Francesca, and Raoul.

Thinking of the Conde with a sense of loss, she wondered what his reactions would be when he discovered she had gone. He had underestimated her if he thought she was prepared to wait in submission for him to ravage her. She half-smiled bitterly. *Ravage!* That was a strange word to use, an old-fashioned word, not at all in keeping with the modern ideas that the Conde implemented.

A rabbit ran across the road in front of the Landrover, and Toni almost jumped out of her skin, swerving dangerously. The action seemed to bring her to complete awareness of her situation. It was no use dreaming while she was driving. She would have plenty of time for recriminations in the months to come.

Pareira's outlying districts were approaching, and she glanced again at her watch. It was only two-thirty, at least four hours before any train might be expected. She drove to the station yard and parked the vehicle, hoping no curious policeman might wonder what she was doing at this hour of the morning. Then she settled down to wait, lighting a cigarette with fingers grown cold from gripping the wheel.

There is nothing more soul-destroying than being

awake during those dead early hours before daybreak. The whole world seems to be asleep and you are the only conscious being. She watched the sun dimpling the sky with a hazy pinkish glow, and felt the unwanted press of tears against her eyes. This was probably the last sunrise she would ever see in Portugal. That accounted for the heavy desolation she was experiencing.

Leaving the Landrover, she carried her cases across to the station barrier where a sleepy Portuguese was opening the gate.

'Excuse me, do you speak English?'

The man surveyed her negligently. 'A little.'

'Then – could you tell me – when may I catch a train to Lisbon?'

The man glanced at the station clock. 'In an hour,' he said, shrugging his shoulders. 'Do you have a ticket?'

Toni shook her head. 'Get a cup of coffee while you wait,' he grunted, and she nodded thankfully and walked across to the buffet.

The train was late, and although she knew she could not possibily have been missed yet, she was a mass of nerves, continually glancing over her shoulder to see if anyone was following her, watching her. She only succeeded in drawing attention to herself, and she thought that very probably the station ticket collector thought she was a trifle mad.

She arrived in Lisbon after lunch, hot and tired and depressed. The train had stopped at every small pass and station on the way, and the sun had burned through the window relentlessly. She went into the station buffet and had a sandwich and some more coffee. She wasn't particularly hungry, but the faintness she was feeling was due in no small part to her emptiness.

She also found some coins and rang the airport. They could offer her a flight late that evening if she could take it. She accepted gladly. At least the speed would save her from having to pay a night's lodging out of her meagre resources.

She spent the afternoon in the shade of the National Library, and took a taxi out to the airport after another snack meal. By now she could hardly keep her eyes open, and the cases were growing heavier every second. The airport lights were bright and unrelenting, and she sat waiting for her flight to be called like a sleepwalker. But once she was ensconced in her seat, she relaxed completely and allowed oblivion to wipe away temporarily all her anxieties.

The stewardess did not wake her until they were landing at London Airport, and by then Toni felt totally numb.

CHAPTER NINE

MRS. MORRIS was astonished to see her. 'Why, Miss Morley,' she exclaimed, 'I understood you was to be away at least six months, didn't I?'

Toni sighed. It was very early in the morning. She had hung about the airport, giving her landlady time to get up and about, but she had not expected this almost cool welcome.

'The job folded,' said Toni dryly. 'What's wrong? Have you re-let the room?'

'No – at least, in a manner of speaking, miss.'

Toni felt overwhelmingly tired. 'What do you mean, Mrs. Morris? In a manner of speaking?'

Mrs. Morris folded her arms across her narrow chest. 'Well, it's like this, you see, miss: my daughter Sandra has left her husband. They've had a row, you know how it is with young people, and I've let her have your room.'

'I see.' Toni hunched her shoulders. 'I see. And my things?' There had been a few books and photographs, things she had kept for sentimental reasons after the house was sold on her parents' death.

'I put them in that big trunk, miss, in the cupboard under the stairs, like. I wasn't to know you'd come haring back without any notice, was I?' Her tone was slight belligerent now.

Toni felt awfully alone. Her room had always seemed

like an oasis in a sea of troubles. Now even it had been taken away from her.

'No, Mrs. Morris,' she said wearily, 'you weren't to know.' She glanced round. 'Have you another room?'

'Not right now, I haven't. There's a gentleman in number ten, he might be moving out in a couple of days – you could have his room.'

'And until he does? What do you suggest I do?'

Mrs. Morris grunted. 'I'm sure I don't know, miss. Couldn't you go to a hotel or something? I mean, you just coming back from Portugal like that with everything found for you – you can't be exactly broke, can you, miss?'

Toni wanted to cry. She wanted to storm at Mrs. Morris and tell her she had no right to let her room without her permission when she was still paying for it, that she had no right to touch her things, pushing them into a trunk in a cupboard under the stairs. But she was much too tired and unhappy. Picking up her cases again, she shook her head and walked out of the door without another word. Mrs. Morris shouted after her:

'Do you want Mr. Bentley's room, then, if he goes?'

Toni did not look back. She felt like a displaced person and she was afraid if she spoke any more to Mrs. Morris she would break down altogether and make a complete ass of herself. So she walked away, caught a bus to Victoria Station and left her cases in the left luggage office while she went out to look for a job and for somewhere to live.

Late in the afternoon she found both. A young professional couple living in a flat in Bayswater required a nanny for their three-year-old daughter, Susan. The agency had already sent three nannies along, all of whom the Masons, as the couple were called, had found unsuitable. They wanted someone young, and Toni fitted the bill. She was employed on a trial basis for a period of one month, given quite a comfortable room of her own with a television set and her own bathroom, and only the child Susan to care for. Other staff were kept and Toni supposed it was quite a sinecure.

Indeed, in the days that followed, calm and comparatively happy days, she managed to restore some of her old confidence, and the Masons were not a difficult couple to work for. Diana Mason was a fashion model, and as she was quite startlingly good-looking, Toni thought with relief that her husband was hardly likely to take a fancy to Susan's nanny with such a glamorous creature for a wife. Despite her looks, Diana was warm and friendly, and it did not take her long to discover that her new governess was not as calm and well-organized as she might be. Something in Toni's wide, sometimes hurt eyes, told her that the girl had suffered some emotional upheaval, and recently. When tentatively questioned, Toni became silent and withdrawn, and Diana gave her a thoughtful appraisal, without probing any more deeply into the matter. Toni was relieved. She had no desire to bare her heart to anyone.

Susan was small, red-haired and good-natured in the main. Occasionally she threw paddies of rage, but these were only very occasional. Andrew Mason was a solicitor, with a thriving practice. They were a very well-ordered and well-balanced family, and Toni thanked her lucky stars for delivering her into their hands, so to speak. The atmosphere in the Masons' flat was soothing to her peace of mind, and within a couple of weeks she had settled down completely.

If she ever gave herself time to think about Raoul, it was with a feeling of dread that one day he might find her and take his revenge, but mostly she assumed that her departure had severed their connection completely. Sometimes she was tempted to ask Andrew Mason whether he had heard of the prosecution of Paul Craig by a Portuguese Count, and then she practically scoffed at her own stupidity. How could she ask a question like that?

And yet it troubled her not a little, and as the days passed and it stayed in her mind, she wondered whether if she phoned him she would be able to set her mind at rest.

One evening, while the Masons were at the theatre, she could stand it no longer, and finding his number in the phone book she dialled his flat. A girl answered, and Toni said: 'Is – is Paul Craig there?'

'Who's calling?' The girl sounded cool.

'A friend,' replied Toni shortly. 'Is he there?'

'Yes, he's here. Do you want to speak to him?'

Did she? *Did she?* Toni hesitated. 'I – er – yes, please.'

There was the sound of a muffled argument, and then Paul came on the line. 'Look, who is this?'

'It's me – Toni Morley.'

'Toni! Saints preserve us! Where the hell have you been?'

'Where have *I* been?' Toni gasped. 'You must know where I've been.'

'You disappeared, three weeks ago you disappeared!'

'How do you know?'

There was the sound of Paul gasping. 'How do I know? God help us, *how do I know?* I know – because I have had my dear uncle breathing fire down my ear ever since!'

'*Raoul!*' murmured Toni faintly.

'Raoul?' echoed Paul. 'So it's Raoul, is it?'

'Oh, stop it, Paul,' exclaimed Toni uncomfortably. 'But – but you must tell me: has – has your uncle threatened to prosecute you?'

'To *prosecute* me?' Paul sounded astounded. 'Hell, he's threatened practically every blasted thing – but prosecution? *No!* Why in God's name should he want to prosecute me? It's not my fault you disappeared!'

'No – but – the money! What about the money?'

'What money?'

'You know. The money Raoul gave you when you left Estrada.'

'Oh, that money!' Paul sounded pleased. 'Yes, never known old Raoul be so generous! He must have wanted to get rid of me pretty badly!'

Toni seemed to be getting nowhere. 'Is – has he gone back? To Portugal?'

'No, not yet. Why?'

'Just curious,' replied Toni, trembling a little.

'Hey, what's your address anyway?' exclaimed Paul swiftly. 'For heaven's sake, don't hang up without giving me your address!'

'Why?'

'For Uncle Raoul, of course. He wants – to see you.'

'Well, I don't want to see him,' replied Toni shortly. So he had been deceiving her all along. He had never had any intention of prosecuting Paul. 'Good-bye, Paul.'

'No – hey, Toni—' But Toni had replaced her receiver, and for a moment she sat staring at it, feeling that old yet familiar sense of apprehension assail her. Had she been a fool to come back to London, to somewhere he was bound to look for her, if that was really why he had come? She should have gone to Leeds, or Birmingham, or even Glasgow. Anywhere far away from his probing mind. It seemed that fate had been on her side when Mrs. Morris let her daughter have her room. Had she been there, he would have found her by now, and then – then – *what*?

The weather in England was getting much colder. Autumn had arrived with a vengeance, and the streets were littered with fallen leaves. Toni took Susan to the Zoo, and they stood, muffled in thick coats and scarves watching the bears in the bear-pit. Toni found herself wondering what it would be like to have a child of her own to take to the Zoo. It would all depend, of course, on who might be the father of that child, and as she was never likely to get married now anyway, she supposed she would never know.

They arrived back at the Bayswater apartments in

the late afternoon, their faces flushed with the cold. Diana was at home and let them in, smiling merrily.

'Oh, hi, darling,' she said to Susan. 'Did you have a good time?'

'Yes, Mummy, we saw all the animals,' said Susan excitedly, as Toni helped her off with her coat. 'Can we go again?'

'Maybe, darling, later. Toni, there's someone here to see you!'

Toni almost felt the blood drain out of her face, leaving her face defenceless, and strangely vulnerable. Diana caught her arm. 'Toni?' she exclaimed. 'What's wrong? What are you afraid of?'

Toni shook her head. 'Nothing – nothing. Who – who is it, Mrs. Mason?'

Diana frowned. 'Well, actually, darling, he says he's a count.'

Toni wanted to turn and run, and then the lounge door opened and Raoul stood there, just looking at her, and she knew her running days were over.

'Well, Toni,' he said huskily, 'at last I've found you!'

Diana looked from one to the other of them, and then taking Susan's resisting hand drew her away, and out of sight. Toni began to remove her coat, but the Conde said harshly: 'Wait, we will go out. We can't talk here!'

Toni bent her head, shivering in spite of the heat of the apartment, and he went to get his overcoat. When he came back he was wearing a thick astrakhan coat over his dark suit and looked disturbingly attractive. Toni saw he was thinner than she remembered, the lines on his face deeper and the scar more revealing.

Without speaking he ushered her out of the apartment, down the stairs and out into the darkening twilight of an October afternoon. They crossed the court before the block of luxury apartments and he opened the door of a dark green car which she recognized as being an Aston Martin. He helped her in, then walked round and slid in beside her. It was the first time they had been alone in a car together, and his thigh brushed hers, sending an electric vibration up her spine.

He set the car in motion, driving expertly out of the parking area and on to the main thoroughfare. Then he turned east, concentrating on the traffic. Toni had plenty of time to study him, and wonder just what his intentions were now.

Eventually he reached a small park near the river, drew the car into the parking area, and stopped. Then he drew out his cigarettes, offered her one, and when she refused, lit one for himself before speaking. When he did speak, his voice was a trifle thick.

'Why did you do it?' he muttered, staring at her intently.

'I suppose you mean – my leaving?'

'Of course!' His accent was more pronounced.

She shrugged. 'You know why, if you think about it. You had no intention of – of prosecuting Paul! You were just using that as a threat to keep me in Estrada!'

She looked blindly out of the car window, unable to speak about such things without becoming emotionally disturbed.

'Did you never wonder why I should go to such lengths to keep you there,' he exclaimed, half angrily. 'Toni, damn you, look at me!'

Toni continued to look out of the window. 'You told me why you were keeping me there, remember? I didn't have to wonder about that!'

'And you believed that – of me?'

She swung round. 'What do you mean – I believed that of you? Of course I believed it! You *meant* it!'

He drew on his cigarette deeply. 'If I had meant it, do you imagine you would still be—' He swore angrily. 'Toni – I wanted you, God, how I wanted you! Do you imagine I would have denied myself as I have done if I really thought you were so – so – well, experienced?'

Toni's legs turned to water. 'What – what do you mean? Oh, I don't understand all this.'

'No,' he agreed tautly, 'you do not!'

She bent her head. Her hair was fastened in the knot on top of her head and the nape of her neck was bare and appealing. With a muffled exclamation, he bent his head, his mouth seeking that gentle curve. 'Oh, God, Toni,' he groaned, 'what have you done to me!'

Toni looked up as he straightened, seeing the naked passion in his eyes, 'Raoul?' she murmured brokenly, 'you're not making sense!'

'Am I not?' he exclaimed roughly, stubbing out his cigarette with hands which were not quite steady. Toni had never seen him like this before. He had always been so calm and detached, except when he was making love to her, and even then she had had the feeling he was merely allowing his passions to take the place of genuine emotion. 'What do you want me to say?' he muttered. 'Surely it's painfully obvious what is wrong with me!'

Toni shook her head. She wanted to believe what her own emotions were telling her was the truth, yet she couldn't. Too much had happened. Too many mistakes had been made. How could anything good come out of this tangle?

Raoul caught her by the shoulders. 'All right, all right,' he said, forcing himself to speak rationally. 'You deserve some explanation, I know. But first, please, tell me I was not wrong: you do love me a little, don't you, Toni?'

Toni's mouth was dry. 'Why – why should I give you that satisfaction?' she asked unsteadily.

'*Por deus!*' he muttered, pulling her savagely towards him. 'This is why!'

His mouth fastened on hers with violent passion, all his pent-up emotions destroying his natural reservations. He had kissed her before, but never with such feeling, his body trembling in her arms. His fingers tore the pins out of her hair so that it fell in silky glory about her shoulders, and he buried his face in its softness. 'You see how it is with me,' he said thickly. 'This is like nothing I have ever known before. I love you, I need you, I can't live without you! I've been half out of my mind these last weeks not knowing where you were, who you were with!'

Toni tried to be sensible. 'You – you've been looking for me?' she murmured tentatively.

'Searching for you,' he amended grimly, drawing

back to look at her. 'As I have been searching since the day you left!'

'But why? Why? Why couldn't you just let me go? You have Laura—'

'Do not mention Laura's name to me!' he said coldly. 'We have discovered we have nothing in common!' She sensed the hauteur in his voice, and shivered a little. 'She spoke to you, did she not, the day you left Estrada?'

Toni nodded her head.

'Louisa revealed that she had paid you a visit. It was strange that she should leave before my mother and Francesca returned. I have seen Laura and have had the truth from her!'

For a moment, Toni pitied Laura. She had believed she had so much, yet she had nothing.

'How – how did you find me?' she asked.

He looked at her, his dark eyes savage. 'In a moment. First, I must explain a few things. I must begin that day in Lisbon, when I almost knocked you down with my car. I was so angry with you, and you were so – well, different from the women of my acquaintance. I was attracted to you, and I half believed you were attracted to me!' He drew out his cigarettes and lit one before continuing. 'You may not believe this, but the following day I went to your hotel to inquire about you. When I discovered you had gone, I was furiously angry with myself for not attempting to see you earlier.' His eyes narrowed. 'The owner told me your name was Senhorita Morley, Senhorita Antonia Morley!'

'Then you knew—'

'Right from the beginning! When I found you at Estrada posing as Paul's fiancée, I was incensed. I had thought you – well, above that kind of escapade. Then when Laura told me she had seen you at the de Calles' I was even more curious.'

'Was that why – you went to Lisbon?'

'Yes. Only to come back and find you ill, after the accident! You cannot conceive my feelings at that time. I wanted to hurt you, badly, not only for deceiving me, but for proving to be – or so I thought – the kind of woman to play around with a man like Miguel de Calle!'

'But that was never true!' exclaimed Toni desperately.

'I know that now. But I will come to that later. At that time I was only concerned with the facts as I saw them, and they added up to a pretty miserable picture. It was then, when I saw you lying there, so helpless and alone, that I realized my feelings for you were more than mere desire for your body!' Toni's cheeks burned. 'So I decided to teach you a lesson, and in the process discover for myself whether you were as black as you had been painted! I knew when I touched you you were not indifferent to me, and maybe some inner sense warned me you could not be the woman I thought you. In any event, I had to keep you at the *castelo*, to see you, to speak with you, to spend time with you. If, by threatening you with the kind of relationship you were afraid of I could punish you, I was human enough to do so. I had been hurt, and this was a new experience for me.'

'So you made me Francesca's governess.'

He half-smiled. 'An inspiration, believe me.'

'And Paul?'

The smile disppeared. 'Laura told you about Elise?'

'Yes.'

'Then you will understand my feelings towards Paul. Elise and I were not lovers, in the truest sense of the word, we were friends who lived together. It was for Francesca that I fought for our marriage.' He shrugged. 'Paul was not serious, I could see that, but Elise would not believe me.' He sighed. 'But that is in the past now. What matters is our future, Toni!' He stubbed out the cigarette. 'I used Paul, I admit it, to keep you at Estrada, but only because I was afraid you might leave me, despite your real feelings. You – you do love me, Toni?'

Toni ran her tongue over her dry lips. 'Yes, I love you,' she said tightly. 'But I'll never live with you!'

Even in the gloom, she could see the haggard expression her words brought to his face. '*Deus*,' he muttered, 'why? Toni, why?'

'I – I'm only human, too,' she whispered. 'I want a home, a real home with a real relationship. Children!'

'And these are things I cannot offer you? Is that it?'

'Well, can you?' Toni stared at him.

'Of course. If the *castelo* does not appeal to you, we can live in Lisbon—'

'Raoul, don't, don't!' She put her hands over her ears.

He looked horrified. 'Is marriage to me so repugnant?' he groaned. 'Does this scar repulse you? Even though you attempt to deny it?'

She could not believe her ears. *'Marriage!'* she breathed. 'You're talking about – *marriage*!'

'What else?' His expression cleared. 'My God, Toni, I really believe you thought I meant something else!'

'I did – I did.' Toni felt the tears rolling down her cheeks.

'You are mad! Quite mad!' he muttered shakily, and pulled her close to him. 'But I deserve it. Forgive me, forgive me!'

She wound her arms round his neck, clinging to him helplessly, until he said a trifle thickly: 'Toni, I am only a man, and I want you very badly. Don't make it impossible for me to let you go!'

Toni flushed, but it was a warm tender flush of colour that lit her face to even greater beauty. 'Oh, Raoul,' she said, 'I adore you, and I'll marry you, whenever you say.'

'Soon, it must be soon,' he murmured caressingly. 'I need a holiday, and we will take it together, hmm?'

'Oh, yes, yes. But how did you find me?' She wanted to know every detail now. She almost laughed when she remembered how nervously she had awaited his revenge, but such sweet revenge.

He lay back in his seat. 'When Francesca found the note she telephoned me at once. Unfortunately I was not in the office, and it was not until the following day that I heard you had gone. Had she been able to find me that day I should have been able to intercept you at the airport. As it was, I merely had confirmation from the flight office that you had left the night before. I took an immediate flight to London, obtaining your address from the de Calles. That was when I challenged Miguel again about his association with you. We were alone, and he actually boasted a little of his conquest.' He uttered a savage expletive. 'He did not boast for long. I could not keep my hands off him.'

Toni pressed closer to him. 'Go on!'

'In London your landlady told me you had acted very strangely because she had let her daughter have your room. After that, I was sunk. So it became a marathon of walking from agency to agency, trying to find you. Paul had no idea where you were, and it was not until today that I found the agency which had supplied the Masons as your employers. I drove straight to the apartment, as you will have guessed. Mrs. Mason was very polite and understanding, although I do not really think she believed that I was a count. I must have seemed very angry and distraught, as indeed I was!' He sighed. 'Even now, I cannot believe the waiting is all over. Don't ever do that to me again, Toni. I do not think I could stand it again!'

Toni reached up to kiss his cheek. 'And Francesca, what will she say?'

He half-smiled. 'Francesca can be in no doubt as to the extent of my feelings for you,' he said, caressing her cheek with his tanned fingers. 'I was like a man possessed when I visited Estrada a week ago to find out whether they had had any word of you.'

'Will she mind?' Toni was persistent.

'I do not think so. She has been a lonely child. It will

be as well when she has brothers and sisters to care for!'

Toni's smile dimpled her cheeks. 'It sounds wonderful,' she murmured.

'It will be,' he promised her, as he started the car, and Toni was glad to leave everything to him.

HARLEQUIN READER SERVICE is your passport to The Heart of Harlequin . . .

if <u>You</u>...

♥ enjoy the mystery and adventure of romance then you should know that Harlequin is the World's leading publisher of Romantic Fiction novels.

♥ want to keep up to date on all of our new releases, eight brand new Romances and four Harlequin Presents, each month.

♥ are interested in valuable re-issues of best-selling back titles.

♥ are intrigued by exciting, money-saving jumbo volumes.

♥ would like to enjoy North America's unique monthly Magazine "Harlequin" — available ONLY through Harlequin Reader Service.

♥ are excited by anything new under the Harlequin sun.

then...

YOU should be on the Harlequin Reader Service — INFORMATION PLEASE list — it costs you nothing to receive our news bulletins and intriguing brochures. Please turn page for news of an EXCITING FREE OFFER.

a Special Offer for <u>You</u>...

just by requesting information on Harlequin Reader Service with absolutely no obligation, we will send you a "limited edition" copy, with a new, exciting and distinctive cover design — **VIOLET WINSPEAR'S** first Harlequin Best-Seller

LUCIFER'S ANGEL

You will be fascinated with this explosive story of the fast-moving, hard-living world of Hollywood in the 50's. It's an unforgettable tale of an innocent young girl who meets and marries a dynamic but ruthless movie producer. It's a gripping novel combining excitement, intrigue, mystery and romance.

A complimentary copy is waiting for YOU — just fill out the coupon on the next page and send it to us to-day.

Don't Miss...

any of the exciting details of The Harlequin Reader Service—**COLLECTOR'S YEAR** . . .

♥ It promises to be one of the greatest publishing events in our history and we're certain you'll want to be a part of it

♥ Learn all about this great new series

♥ Reissues of some of the earliest, and best-selling Harlequin Romances

♥ All presented with a new, exciting and distinctive cover design

To become a part of the Harlequin Reader Service **INFORMATION PLEASE** list, and to learn more about **COLLECTOR'S YEAR** — simply fill in the coupon below and you will also receive, with no obligation, LUCIFER'S ANGEL, by Violet Winspear.

SEND TO: ➡ Harlequin Reader Service,
"Information Please",
M.P.O. Box 707,
Niagara Falls, New York 14302.

CANADIAN RESIDENTS ➡ Harlequin Reader Service,
Stratford, Ont., Can.   N5A 6W4

Name _____

Address _____

City _____ State/Prov. _____

Zip/Postal Code _____

IP 306